GETTING LINCOLN'S GOAT

AN ELLIOT ARMBRUSTER MYSTERY

E. M. GOLDMAN

A YEARLING BOOK

Published by
Bantam Doubleday Dell Books for Young Readers
a division of
Bantam Doubleday Dell Publishing Group, Inc.
1540 Broadway
New York, New York 10036

ISBN: 0-440-41332-X

Reprinted by arrangement with Delacorte Press

Printed in the United States of America

May 1997

10 9 8 7 6 5 4 3 2 1

OPM

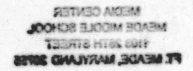

CHAPTER ONE

IT WAS THE KIND OF NIGHT when neon signs whisper false promises to those who dream. The city streets were shining like a pair of cheap black shoes—the ones that go with the school band uniform and the pasted-on smile.

Somewhere beyond the megastory skyscrapers, galaxies were forming. In the alleyway of lost hopes, rain trickled down my neck, streaking my glasses, while rats played peek-a-boo with each other and yesterday's newspaper turned to mush in the gutter.

I'm Elliot Armbruster. I carry a clarinet.

"You look like a drowned ferret," said Dan McGrew, talking out of the corner of his mouth in the way he does on TV. "Are you sure you want to be here, Elliot? Wouldn't you rather be in your life skills class? That's where you're supposed to be."

"Th—this is great," I sputtered. "Honest, Dan. If I can be of any help in rescuing the girl—"

"You're okay, kid." He patted my shoulder almost absentmindedly. I hugged closer to the loaded Dumpster, trying to look like another garbage bag, staying out of sight. I stumbled over some loose trash but caught myself before I could fall. A stench rose around us, reminding me of things that had died and nobody wanted to recycle.

We were watching a third-floor window in the brick building across the street, where the bald man was meeting the blonde. She was really on our side, collecting information to clear her brother of a murder rap. Lola was sixteen and taking big chances with guys who didn't always play fair.

Dan and I were carrying guns even though Dan doesn't approve of kids packing artillery. My gun was black licorice. It looked real as long as the light was dim enough and it didn't pick up too much fluff from my jacket pocket. I hoped the gun wasn't getting wet or I'd be in a real mess, in more ways than one. "When are we going to rush them?" I asked.

"Be patient."

Dan is always saying that. He's promised that when I turn sixteen and get my learner's permit, I can drive the Mercedes sometime when we have to leave in a hurry. Only I won't be sixteen for months. I don't see how I can wait that long. Dan says that standing around in the rain with your clothes sticking to your skin is a good way to practice patience. Tonight I was getting enough practice to last until I was a senior.

All at once Dan gripped my shoulder hard. A window shade was being pulled down in the apartment we were watching, then it went up again. Our signal to move. "Listen to me carefully, Elliot—"

• • •

2

"Elliot. *Elliot*—" I looked up and almost groaned. Ms. Winston stood so close to my desk that her foot was touching my clarinet case. From her expression I could tell that she'd asked me a question. This was Grade 10 Life Skills, which she's been teaching since they built the school around her thirty years ago.

She'd been saying something about the importance of choosing the right career. "I guess it's important to choose the right career," I said, fumbling for words, "because it's something you're going to be doing for a long time. At least until you get to die or retire."

This was obviously not the question she had asked, but she didn't look too unhappy. "Then you may wish to consider your answer for a few more minutes. Not that your choice is binding." She chuckled, so everyone else chuckled, too. Her expression grew serious. "After all, this is supposed to be a learning experience."

"Okay." I hate being first, but it happens a lot when your name starts with *A*. I never noticed Janice Aldridge until she transferred out. Then I really missed old Jan, if you know what I mean. Sometimes I can talk in class and the words come out okay. Other times I end up sounding like a tape that got dropped and stepped on by somebody with gum on his shoes.

Ms. Winston returned to the front of the class. "Maybe today we should start from the other end of the alphabet. Paulette Zak. Paulette, what career do you plan to pursue?"

I want to be a history teacher. I mouthed the words along with her.

Lester, this guy who sits behind me, hit my shoulder so hard that I almost fell onto my open notebook. "Hey,

3

dork," he said in a low voice. "What happened? Did you fall asleep?"

"I had a hard night." I tried to make it sound as if I'd been doing something more interesting than watching *Dangerous Dan McGrew*, my favorite TV detective show. Like maybe I was with a girl and we weren't just friends.

Lester snickered. "In your dreams. Just now you lucked out."

"Francine Raines," Ms. Winston called. I had gone to kindergarten with Francie, who hasn't changed much since then. She still has carroty red hair and a pale complexion. Her face and her arms and legs are heavily sprinkled with very dark freckles, like you're supposed to take a pen and connect the dots.

"I want to be a lawyer," Francie answered so softly that I could hardly hear her.

She's always been like that. Even when she was five, she was whispery. She also still acts like she's trying to be invisible even when nobody is looking. I can sympathize.

Ms. Winston nodded encouragingly. "Your mother is a trial lawyer, isn't she?"

Francie bit her lip. "Yes." Ms. Winston looked like she was about to call on the next person. Then Francie spoke up again, her voice stronger this time. "Or maybe I'll be somebody who works to protect the Amazon rain forests." When a couple of people laughed, her face went red. She backtracked quickly. "No, definitely a lawyer. A lawyer. I'm sure. Like my mom. But maybe not for trials."

I think she had remembered what we had to do for the rest of the assignment. Each of us had to find out information about a job we might get later. Ms. Winston says it's never too early for us to plan for our future. We had a month to hand in an essay based on personal re-

4

search. The thousand-word essay would be worth half our grade for the term.

My folks always want me to bring up my grades in all my classes, although I personally don't think my grades are that bad. Okay, I don't achieve my potential. Other than some genius who enters Yale at age ten, who does?

I wonder what Dangerous Dan was doing when he was fifteen. I bet his folks never told him to pull up his grade average. Not that *I* think that I watch too much TV, but my mom is threatening to cut down my viewing hours until my grades improve. She's worried that I might be living in a fantasy world.

Ms. Winston continued to call on people. "Dana Radford—"

"A dancer." That big surprise came from a girl who spends half her life in a tutu.

Somebody else wanted to be a history teacher.

The answers were all predictable even though Ms. Winston had announced at the start of the term that we were all going on a voyage of personal discovery. Spreading our sails. Expanding our horizons. Each time somebody answered *I want to be a history teacher,* kissing noises would come from a couple of guys sitting near the back.

Those who didn't want to teach history wanted to do what their parents did.

"A cook."

"A secretary."

"Bruno?"

"Huh?" That was Bruno Maros, the biggest and oldest kid in class because he got held back once. This is a guy who looks like he should shave twice a day.

She sighed. "What do you want to be?"

Bruno usually takes a while to answer, only this time I didn't think he was going to say anything. He sat there, looking first up at the ceiling, then down at the floor. "A carpenter," he said at last, not sounding too happy about it.

"Like Jesus," Lester whispered. He went on in case I didn't get it. "Jesus was a carpenter."

Bruno was not going to be Jesus. Although he wasn't a bully, this is not a guy you'd expect to turn the other cheek. That would be obvious even if he wasn't wearing military fatigues and didn't have his hair practically shaved off. Bruno is the only kid I know who keeps copies of *Soldier of Fortune* in his locker. I've never read the magazine, but I had the impression that *Soldier of Fortune* was to Bruno what the *TV Guide* was to me. Rumor had it that he'd prefer hand-to-hand combat to a date with the Playmate of the Month—unless she was carrying an Uzi.

Bruno's dad and all his uncles are in the construction trade, so I figured that they expected him to join the family business.

Speaking of families, my father is an actuary. My mom fills out tax forms for H&R Block. My parents have been hinting that I should become an accountant like my cousin Michael, who might be able to find me a job in his CPA firm if I bring up my grades and get into a good college and then graduate. It's never too early to start thinking about what you're going to be doing seven years from now, right?

I'd figured out my parents' message a long time ago: Achieve your potential, but don't take any chances.

Whenever Bruno straightens up in his chair, it creaks. Ms. Winston started to go on, except that there was this noise like Bruno's desk was coming apart. "Ms. Winston—"

"Yes, Bruno?"

He had a hopeless look on his face. "How about if I say I want to be something else instead? Just for in here." You could see he was struggling for words. "I mean, I know I'm going to be a carpenter because it's all set up for me to apprentice with my uncle Dom and everything."

"I'd like each of you to examine careers that might interest you." Ms. Winston nodded encouragingly. "This is the time when you should be looking around, exploring yourselves."

I saw Lester gaze around to see who was watching. Ms. Winston was making these encouraging noises at Bruno, and Bruno was staring down at his desk. Then Lester scratched himself and lifted his shirt sleeve like he was finding a bug and squashing it.

I got it. He was exploring himself.

"Aw, forget it," Bruno mumbled. "My dad's got everything set up."

"There's no harm in looking—" She broke off because it was obvious that Bruno was no longer listening.

She called on a few more people. There was another secretary. A long-distance trucker. A guy whose parents run a funeral home said he wanted to be either a forensic pathologist or a meat packer.

"A history teacher." That was Lester, whose last name is Davis. Ms. Winston's smile began to look strained and the kissing noises had stopped. My turn was coming up soon.

"I don't like to be the bearer of bad tidings," Ms. Winston said stiffly. "But there are only so many positions available for history teachers."

7

"Darn," Lester said, and the guys at the back laughed. I didn't.

Maybe I should explain why so many people wanted to be history teachers. Every year Ms. Winston gives out the same assignment. You have to choose what you want to be and interview somebody in that occupation. Mr. Hardy is a history teacher. He doesn't like kids wasting his time, so he has this handout ready for anybody who has to write Ms. Winston's assignment. All the facts are there—education, duties, the whole thing.

Out of twenty-five kids in class, so far there were seven who said they hoped to be history teachers. Setting sails toward Mr. Hardy's classroom. Expanding their horizons all the way down the hall.

I was going to make it eight, and I think she knew it. "Elliot, have you come to a decision?" She had already started writing on her clipboard.

See, I have this reputation. Or maybe it's that I don't have a reputation. I can always be counted on to say something harmless. I think it's the glasses—Clark Kent had everybody fooled, too. Only with me, I can see myself taking off the suit and the glasses and finding another suit and another pair of glasses underneath. "Elliot? Do you have an occupation you want to explore?"

A history teacher. That's what I planned to say. Three words. Never mind that I'd rather have my fingernails torn out than stand up in front of a class and give a long speech. No, I definitely did not want to be a history teacher.

She was waiting. "Elliot?"

Lester jabbed his pencil into my back. "Hey, have you died or something?" His voice rose. "Ms. Winston, Elliot already said he wants to be a history teacher." Her lips went together as if she was about to shush him. "Like me."

Before I could change my mind, I spoke up. "A private eye." Each word came out loud, crystal clear. "I want to be a private investigator."

First there was dead silence. Then:

Oooooooooooooooooooh. It was like the room was sighing.

I could tell right away that speaking out had not been such a good idea. A lot of guys in the room were sitting up and grinning at each other. So were some of the girls. Behind me, Lester was pounding on his desk.

If I'd laughed right then, I probably could have saved the situation. A joke. All I had to do was say with an absolutely straight face that history was my life.

"Ms. Winston!" Francie was waving her hand wildly. "I really want to go to the Amazon. I *hate* the idea of being a lawyer." Then she looked around as if she didn't know who had spoken.

Ms. Winston was erasing something from her clipboard and writing something else. "A private investigator. And . . . Francine wants to go to the Amazon." She smiled encouragingly. "That sounds fascinating. I'm sure the class will be interested in your reports."

"My report!" Francie sucked in her breath. "That means I have to find—"

"Ms. Winston—" That was Bruno.

She nodded at him.

"A soldier. Infantry." He swallowed. "That's what I'm sort of interested in doing."

"I thought you might be." There was enough of the teacher's clipboard visible so I could see that her list was getting pretty messy. But she didn't look unhappy about

9

the changes. "You know, these days we usually think of soldiers as peacekeepers." She made the military sound like crossing guards helping baby ducks through an intersection. "That's why you want to be a soldier, isn't it, Bruno? To assist with world peace? That's really a very commendable goal."

His next words were spoken in an entirely matter-of-fact way. "I want to learn more ways to kill people."

Ooooooooooooooooooooooooooh.

Ms. Winston stopped writing on her clipboard and her hand went up to touch the pink scarf she was wearing. Then her hand came down again. I don't think she was aware that her pen had left a blue line down the side of her jaw. She smiled brightly. "Of course, soldiers have to be ready, in case of a national emergency. But there are many directions to take in the military—"

He was looking at her like she didn't understand. "I think I'd be really good at killing people. The enemy, I mean. There are all these ways you can do it with your bare hands. Like it only takes two fingers to—"

"Perhaps you can include some of those details in your report." Her voice sounded faint. "But don't feel you have to."

Look, it wasn't as if Bruno said he wanted to be a hit man for the Mob. Or like he was some kind of psycho. I mean, he was probably even going to be on our side.

Ms. Winston had collected herself. "If anyone else changes his or her mind over the next few days, speak to me. Now I'd like to outline the assignment for your interview." She looked up. "Yes, Bruno?"

"That—what I said—it's just for here, right?"

"Right. Incidentally, Bruno, carpentry is a very old and honored profession."

"Jesus was a carpenter." That was Lester.

Bruno frowned. "That was before they had power tools."

Just then the bell rang.

Bruno's like me and Francie in that he usually doesn't say much. People don't notice us because we're just there—except maybe Bruno, who can look fairly scary if you come on him from the wrong direction. All of a sudden the three of us had become interesting.

"You're okay, Armbruster," Bruno said to me as we left the classroom. "Not like the rest of those turkeys." He punched my shoulder by way of emphasis. I almost punched him back.

"*Thanks.*" Francie passed by. She didn't sound like she meant thanks. She was complaining to a friend that her mother expected to help her do research on her brilliant future law career. And now she was going to have to find an environmentalist to interview.

"Do you know any detectives?" Bruno asked. My shoulder was still aching. Between him and Lester, I knew I'd have some A-Number-One bruises.

I shook my head glumly. No doubt about it, now I was in deep dog food. Everything I knew about PIs came from TV. These guys were always investigating criminals and rescuing people. If I had trouble mumbling answers in class, I could just see myself dialing a stranger's number from the phone book. *Hi, I'm a kid and I want to interview you when you're not busy dodging bullets.*

Maybe it wasn't too late to say that I had changed my mind. Maybe I could convince Ms. Winston that it was a tough decision, but more than anything I wanted to make kids memorize the order of the presidents.

I almost missed the next thing Bruno said. "Tell you

what. If you help me with my paper, I'll introduce you to my uncle Devlin."

"Your uncle?"

"Yeah. He's a private eye."

After life skills we had a pep rally outside to cheer for our dynamic football team, the Lincoln Leopards.

For band members the rallies are a command performance. For everybody else they're more or less voluntary since attendance isn't taken. Everyone is supposed to want to go, but mostly the football fans show up and all the younger kids. The smokers go off to coat their lungs, some couples try for a little unsupervised time together. You get the idea. However, because this year's team was strong, almost everyone came.

My mind was definitely not on my music. In fact, Mr. Silverberg told me later that when I'm sick, I should tell him so I can be excused from playing.

I was going to meet a private investigator.

My mind also was not on the rally. I barely noticed when they trotted out the school mascot, an Angora goat with a blanket on his back in the Lincoln High School colors (gold and green). Somebody had also draped a leopard skin over the blanket—not a real one, of course, or the Animal Rights Club would have a fit.

I was going to meet a private investigator.

The crowd went wild on cue when the school president hung a garland around the goat's neck. The cheerleaders turned cartwheels in their green-and-gold outfits. The goat regarded them curiously.

The goat wasn't going to meet a real detective.

CHAPTER TWO

"**B**UT HE'S BRUNO'S UNCLE," I protested. At home things were not going well. "Bruno will be with us."

Mom's mouth was set. "We've never met this man. I can't have you going on a—a stakeout—with a stranger."

"*Surveillance,* Mom. Not a stakeout."

"No matter what you call it, it hardly sounds like a suitable activity for a teenager."

"Oh, I don't know. It might be fun." That was Aunt Sheila. She's twenty-eight, my mother's youngest sister. She teaches English at the local community college.

"It might be dangerous." Mom obviously thought it was time to change the subject. She took a cookbook from the bookshelf and began to leaf through it. "Sheila, I'm trying something new for Friday's dinner. You and Steve should come over." Steve was Aunt Sheila's latest fiancé, a tweedy-jacket type.

I'd heard the grim details of Friday's dinner and I planned to fill up beforehand on peanut butter sandwiches. Aunt Sheila was looking my way, so I pantomimed sticking my finger down my throat.

"I already have other plans," she said. "Sorry."

Since I had just saved my aunt from poisoning, it stood to reason that she owed me. I gave her my best pleading look.

"Lillian," she said mildly, "why don't you telephone Bruno's mother? After all, this detective is a relative. Ask her about him."

Bruno had explained that Devlin McCray was more like an honorary uncle. He and one of Bruno's uncles were good friends in high school, and he lived with the Maros family for a few years after something happened to his own parents.

Mom didn't say anything for a minute. "All right, I will. Elliot—"

"I have Bruno's number," I said quickly.

Mom hung up before she finished dialing. "Maybe I'll make this call from the bedroom."

Aunt Sheila had moved to the dining-room table to correct some school papers. She saw me start toward the hallway. "I bet you won't be able to hear anything."

"I'm just going to the bathroom." Look, a real investigator isn't about to let his mother make a call that concerns his entire future without at least trying to listen. Of course, a real investigator probably doesn't cross his fingers behind his back when he isn't telling the truth.

I couldn't hear much. We have this old house built in the 1920s. Dad's always saying that they don't make 'em like that anymore. Still, Mom's voice carries.

"—something stable. Well, of course. He thinks that it's glamorous. Really? That's marvelous. Oh, yes. I can certainly appreciate—"

I didn't hear what she could certainly appreciate. She was going to let me go with Bruno's uncle Devlin. Great! Only I couldn't hear Mom's voice anymore. I made it to the end of the hallway just as the bedroom door opened, then zoomed into the living room. I grabbed a magazine from the coffee table, opened it, and sat down on the couch in a single fluid motion.

"*Woman's Day*, Elliot?" Aunt Sheila asked softly as Mom came in. I jettisoned it over the side.

Mom was humming. "I want you to know, Mom," I said, "I'll respect your decision, no matter what it is."

Aunt Sheila groaned.

"Elliot—" Mom was looking pleased with herself. "Bruno's mother has convinced me that going on surveillance might be a valuable experience for you."

"Great!" I didn't exactly get up and dance in the middle of the floor, but you get the idea. So it was all set up. We were going out the next day, Saturday, me and Bruno and Devlin McCray. Mom started talking about my homework and reeling off a list of chores I was to accomplish that night, but I didn't care.

"I'm going to get started with my English paper," I said. "Okay if I use the computer?"

I figured on keeping the volume really low so she wouldn't hear the grunts from Aliens A.D. 3000. On the other hand, if Mom caught me playing a computer game, she might change her mind about letting me go. Maybe I really would do the paper early. Then I realized she was saying something. "What?"

"I said you should check first with Sheila to see if she needs to use our computer."

Sheila looked up. "Mine's still operational, believe it or not." Aunt Sheila's computer is compatible with ours, only hers keeps breaking down. "Feel free to use your own machine."

"But no games, Elliot," Mom cautioned.

"Of course not." I think I did a good job of looking offended.

To find out why Mom had changed her mind so quickly about my going with Devlin McCray, I stayed in the hallway. I didn't have to wait long. Aunt Sheila asked Mom why she looked so smug.

"Her brother-in-law handles insurance claims," Mom answered. "He watches people suspected of faking injuries."

I guess she didn't think that sounded very exciting.

Around ten on Saturday morning my mom drove me over to Bruno's house. Devlin McCray definitely wasn't what I expected. For one thing, he's not much taller than I am, and I'm five seven. He has fair hair that he wears a little longer than most guys his age, which I guessed was early thirties. He had on old jeans and a gray sweatshirt. Maybe he did something to keep fit, but his arms weren't exactly bulging with muscles. He looked more like a runner.

What really got to me was that he wore the sort of clothes my dad uses for washing the car. Dangerous Dan wears suits even when he's leaping from one building to another. Great-looking women in evening dresses keep falling all over him. The only time he doesn't wear a suit is when he works out. Whenever he's at the gym pressing weights and sweating, great-looking women in spandex fall all over him.

Devlin has a face that would blend into any crowd. His only distinguishing feature is his nose, which has some bumps like it's been broken a few times. I didn't notice until later that he has eyes like blue lasers.

When he was halfway into the living room, he stopped and stared at Bruno. Then he shook his head and reached out to touch Bruno's marine cut. "How many guys held you down while they did that to you?"

Bruno thought that was pretty funny. Anyway, we stood up. I think I mentioned before that Bruno is over six feet tall. He introduced me to Devlin and we shook hands. I'm not awfully used to shaking hands. Mine was sweating.

"I hope you're not expecting detective work to be anything like on TV," he said right off. "Your mom says you like watching *Dangerous Dan McGrew.*" I owed Mom for that. "I saw that show once. That's just entertainment. Real detective work is a lot more tedious."

"I know there's a lot of waiting around for something to happen," I said.

"That and a lot of phoning around, and a lot of paperwork. I spend a fair amount of time punching a computer and visiting government offices." At least he wasn't laughing at me. "This is for a school project, right? I understand you're helping out Bruno. Are you good in school?"

"I do okay."

"Better than me," Bruno said.

Dev brought a videotape he'd shot. He showed us a few minutes of this guy walking along in a neck brace, then some blown-up stills so we could see his face better. We would be looking for a man in his mid-fifties who was almost bald except for a fringe around the sides and some combed over. On the tape, when the wind blew, the hair on top flopped over. He was walking slowly down the sidewalk. Really slowly.

The drill was this: Devlin was hired by an insurance company to follow this man, whose name was George Russell. He had been in a car accident the previous year and supposedly had a problem with his neck that didn't show up on X rays. Maybe he was telling the truth and maybe he was lying. *Exaggerating* was the word Dev used. He explained that his job was to stay near the subject's house and follow him when he went out. ("Subject" is detective talk.)

Dev says the insurance company keeps hoping he'll get a photo of somebody jumping up out of a wheelchair and turning cartwheels. He says he has a modest success rate in finding phonies. From the way he said it, I didn't think his sympathies were always with the company.

Before we left, he said he was going to use the bathroom. He advised us to do the same. When I had talked to him on the phone, he said to dress inconspicuously and to limit our intake of fluids. I wrote in my notebook: *Detectives do not get potty breaks*.

Bruno's mom had prepared a lunch for all of us. "A picnic basket?" Devlin looked pained as he opened the basket. "This is enough to feed an entire school bus. Evie—"

She shrugged. "Two growing boys and one bachelor. If there are any leftovers, you take them home. And come around more often. Don't be such a stranger."

He sighed. "Okay, Evie."

Picture a day in early November, cool but not very. No serious clouds but not exactly sunbathing weather. Picture three guys on surveillance in a tan sedan. The real detective is in the front seat with a picnic basket that, after two hours, is about two-thirds decimated. In the rearview mirror the detective looks half asleep. In the backseat, one teenage kid is helping another kid twice his size with math.

Before we left, Devlin had said that no matter what, we were to stay where he put us. If something unexpected happened, we might have to take the bus home. Apparently very little unexpected ever happens, but he still made sure that we both had bus fare.

It was okay at first. For the first hour, we just sat there and ate and talked. Then the sun came out, and the car heated up to at least two hundred degrees. Bruno even removed his army jacket. It turns out that this guy has muscles on his muscles from working construction with his uncle. He was wearing a T-shirt underneath (olive green, of course).

Bruno got a few math problems right by himself except that he was starting to nod off. I was beginning to feel like a Thanksgiving turkey. Even though I tried hard not to yawn, at last I did.

"This is just an assignment, right?" Dev said. "You're not actually thinking of becoming a detective. I gather your mother told Bruno's mother—"

"This is homework," I confirmed, evasive. "It sounded interesting."

"Still think it sounds interesting?" All the car windows were cranked down as far as they would go.

Okay, the truth was that what we were doing was not interesting. On TV, you know that the detectives have been sitting around because after the commercial break, they're either stretching or pouring a cup of coffee from a thermos. This was real time. What we were doing was the most boring thing I'd ever done in my entire life.

"Being a detective sounds more interesting than a lot

19

of other things," I said. "I wasn't exactly expecting a thrill every minute." Of course, I'd been hoping . . .

Bruno worked on his math awhile longer, then dropped off. Even Dev was yawning. "Come on," he said, opening his door. "Let's look at the engine." I was about to ask him if something was wrong with the car. "We need an excuse to be hanging around. The neighbors are starting to be suspicious."

"You mean that woman in the blue house?" I had seen the same lady peek through her curtains three times.

"You noticed. Good." His response made me glow, or maybe the sun was getting hotter. Elliot Armbruster, boy detective.

When I got out, one of my feet had gone to sleep, but I decided it would be uncool to stomp. "What about—" I gestured toward Bruno, who was sleeping with his head thrown back and his mouth open. A fly buzzed around lazily.

"Leave Sleeping Beauty where he is." Dev opened his hood and examined the inside. "Yep, everything's all there."

"Do you know very much about engines?" I asked.

"Enough to know that this one will do what I want it to. Gets good mileage, too."

Dan McGrew has this shiny black car that must run on no gas at all because you never see him stopping in the middle of a chase to fuel up. He sure doesn't keep a bunch of gas coupons on the dashboard, or rolls of change for parking meters.

I asked Dev about his background because that information was part of my project. He told me that many private investigators used to be with the police. Some come from the military. Dev started doing security work while he was in college, as a night watchman at a factory. After he graduated, he couldn't find work in the field he'd studied, so he drove an armored car for a while.

There was a stretch when he'd sat in a lobby "baby-sitting" a high-rise office building. He left because he was spending so much time in uniform that he was beginning to feel like an usher. So he did a sort of apprenticeship with an investigation firm. Then he and a buddy split off and formed their own company.

He didn't say what had happened to his friend except that they weren't partners anymore. Now he worked for himself, and he preferred it that way. Dan McGrew is a loner, too.

"What did you want to be?" I asked, curious. Maybe this sounds weird, but even though I was bored—even though we were just hanging around waiting for something to happen—in one part of my brain, I couldn't imagine anything more exciting. It was like buying tickets for a movie you'd been waiting for and getting there early so you could get a good seat. You knew that sooner or later, you were going to see one heck of a show.

"What?" He was staring at his engine. He looked up. "Sorry, Elliot. I was thinking about something else."

"What did you study in college?" Criminology, I assumed. "What was it you wanted to be?"

He shrugged. "I figured I'd teach high school. But there weren't too many jobs for new history graduates." Dev grinned suddenly. "I would have made a lousy teacher. You're lucky that no one hired me."

The old lady had appeared at her window again. Only this time she was talking on the phone. I hoped she wasn't calling the police. "Do you carry a gun?" I asked.

"Sometimes. Depends on the job. Or the neighborhood. Or if I expect to run into trouble."

"Are you carrying a gun now?" He shook his head.

A black pickup pulled up next to us. "Are you having car trouble?" asked a man in a Jays baseball cap. He was in his late twenties, a strong face with a long mustache, black T-shirt. "I noticed you two when I drove by earlier, and here you still are. Need a hand?"

Here we still were, all right.

"I'm waiting for this buddy of mine." Dev made a big show of looking at his watch. "He's a mechanic, and he's been nursing this baby along for the last couple of months. The boys and I are going to sit here awhile longer."

"That make is usually pretty reliable." The guy gripped his steering wheel. "Anyhow, suit yourselves. Good luck!"

"Thanks." Dev watched him drive away until he turned the corner. His voice was soft. "I didn't see him before."

We were on a residential street with light traffic, but that didn't mean no trucks had passed. I was surprised that Dev expected to remember every vehicle that went by. I said so.

"His plates," he said. I looked at him blankly. "The first three letters are ABE. I usually hone in on any license plate that spells out a word or a name, or where there's a sequence."

The car door opened and Bruno got out. He was staggering like he'd just woken up, which he had. "Anything happen yet?"

"Not yet." Dev looked at his watch. "You two boys might as well run along. We've probably had all the excitement we're entitled to today. I'm going to stay for another hour or so."

"Okay if I stay with you awhile longer?" I asked. "I still have to ask a few more questions for my paper." We only had to hand in five typed pages and I already had enough information, but I wanted to know more. For me.

"Suit yourself."

Even though I hadn't been drinking any liquid, I needed to go. I told Dev I was going to make a pit stop at a service station two blocks down, where the street turns onto a shopping area. He barely listened, just kept looking at his engine and twiddling with wires.

The gas station was also near the bus stop, so Bruno and I headed in the same direction. He waited until we were out of earshot before saying anything. "B-O-R-I-N-G. I don't know how Dev does it."

"He has to be patient, I guess."

"Sure, man, but every day? Just sit? Could you do that?"

"I don't know. Maybe if I thought the information I was after was worth it."

He shook his head. "I don't know about you, Armbruster."

After we'd both gone into the men's, we parted company. Bruno planned to visit an army recruiter early in the week, and then we'd work on his paper together. I advised him to go easy on the part about saying he wanted to be a human war machine. Chances were he'd find out more if he asked about career opportunities. It would be good if he said he wanted to serve his country.

Bruno said that made him sound like he wanted to be a waiter. No way, man. He wanted a gun. Better, a tank. He asked me if I wanted to come over to his place to do the paper. He had a copy of *GI Joe: The Movie*. We could watch it together if his mom wasn't around.

"How about if we take out the latest *Meat Cleaver High*?" I suggested. "It's supposed to be available this week."

"You like *Meat Cleaver*?" Bruno looked surprised, which pleased me for some reason.

"I've seen every one at least five times. But maybe we'd better write the paper first."

"Sure. Okay." It turned out Bruno thinks *MCH* is okay. We compared notes about our favorites until he spotted his bus.

For anyone who has somehow missed out on the greatest gross-out series of our time, this is background information contained in the first film, *How I Died During My Summer Vacation*. *MCH* concerns this high school (which some call Beaver Cleaver High, although it's really Milton Carruthers Senior High School).

Once upon a time there was this vice principal nobody liked. On Grad Night a bunch of guys stuffed him into a locker by way of celebration. Then they spun the lock and went off with their girlfriends and forgot all about Mr. Kramer. The only thing was that the school was closed for the whole summer. No janitor, no painters. Nothing.

Anyway, whenever there's a full moon, or a dance, Mr. Kramer's decomposing body walks the halls. And this is a guy who didn't like kids even when he was alive. In Part 1 he comes out of his haunted locker and goes on a vengeance spree, starting with the home ec teacher, who is one of the girls from the original group that did him in. He corners her in her classroom, which comes equipped with everything sharp for slicing and dicing, including a meat cleaver that could split an ox. He starts with the cookie cutters.

I was walking back toward the sedan when it passed me going the other way. "Hey!" I yelled.

Dev saw me and pointed forward. I sprinted and caught up with him in the parking lot of a bowling alley two blocks down.

He explained the situation while I caught my breath. "My background on Mr. Russell says he's an avid bowler, or used to be. He belongs to a group that meets on Saturday." He nodded toward the other side of the lot. "A guy in that green Jeep picked him up. I assume they're already inside."

"Wouldn't it be stupid to go bowling if he was faking?"

"A lot of people, Elliot, are incredibly stupid."

Do you remember how I said I hadn't noticed at first how Dev has eyes like lasers? He gets that way when he's thinking. Only it was scary the first time I saw him like that because he was looking straight at me. He seemed to be debating with himself. "Would you mind doing a small favor for me?" he asked.

"Sure, Dan." Then I realized what I'd said. "Dev, I mean. I mean—what do you want me to do?"

He passed his hand through his hair. For a minute it looked like he'd changed his mind. Then he sighed. "You know how to bowl, right?"

CHAPTER THREE

"**B**OWL? ME?" I think my voice squeaked.

"Right. So I can tape your performance."

"But you'll really be taping Russell while he's bowling."

"Good. You're quick." He was checking his camera.

"Dev?"

"What?"

"I don't know how to bowl."

He sighed again. "Do you have anything against my showing you? Some fundamentals, I mean."

"Okay with me."

Okay? It was great.

When you go into the lobby of the Lucky Strike Lanes, there's an open refreshment area off to the right with round white tables and chairs. Except where the lanes are, the whole place has bright-red flowered carpeting. Through the double doors and just inside the bowling area itself is the counter where you rent shoes and get score sheets.

As soon as Dev came into the main area, he started looking around for Russell, but in a casual way that made it seem like he was looking over the lanes. I recognized one of the girls giving out shoes. Pam Culhane. Pam's on the school paper. She's also president of the Photography Club, which I joined at the start of the term after my granddad gave me his old camera. She's a year older than I am, a junior, with shoulder-length hair somewhere between blond and brown. Very pretty, but she acts almost like she doesn't notice it.

Dev took a pair of shoes from another of the girls behind the counter and went over to put them on. I stayed behind to say hello to Pam.

"Oh, hi, Elliot," she said when she saw me. She has a nice smile. When she turned it on me, I felt it going all the way down, like a hot drink. She has a boyfriend, by the way. A senior. I thought I should mention that up front.

I looked around. "So, you work here."

"Yep, I sure do." She waited. "Do you want shoes?"

"Sure."

"What size?" I had to try on a couple pairs, maybe because the first time I messed up and told her the size I wore last year. I decided I wouldn't like a job where I had to handle other people's smelly shoes. At least my Adidas were fairly new.

By that time there weren't any other people waiting at the counter and the other girl had left. "I heard about what you said in life skills," Pam said. "Speaking out like that takes courage."

"Did you see that guy I'm with?" I motioned for her

to lean forward, then whispered, "He's a detective. We're on an assignment."

"Here?"

I nodded. "Following a guy. Maybe an insurance fraud."

"Which one?"

By then I'd spotted Russell. He was sitting at a table in front of a lane. Several other men were standing around him, talking. One of them was really big. Dev had told me that Russell operated heavy machinery when he was working. Maybe these were guys he worked with, although they all seemed twenty years younger. "He's the balding guy keeping score on lane six. Blue shirt."

"The one with the neck brace?"

I nodded. "Do you know him?" Maybe she'd seen something.

She shook her head. "I think he's been in before. I'm not sure."

When I joined Dev, he was picking out a bowling ball. He seemed to be deliberately spending a lot of time making his choice in the same way he had been fiddling with his car engine. "Cute girl," he remarked when I joined him.

"I know her from school," I said casually. "I asked her if she's seen Russell before. She wasn't sure."

He stiffened. "You didn't tell her—"

"She's cool," I said. I mean, anyone who wants to be a journalist has to be cool, right?

"I hope you're right." He found a ball for me that he said should do okay. Maybe it was the smaller size, but I still felt like I had a million-pound weight hanging off my fingers. He explained that the most important things to remember about the ball were (a) not to drop it on my foot, (b) not to drop it on his foot, (c) not to drop it on the wooden lane, which isn't supposed to have craters, and (d) to release the ball at the proper time so it wouldn't break my fingers or take me with it. Apparently it's cheating to knock down pins with your body.

I'm not totally uncoordinated. It only looks that way when I'm nervous. However, Dev was patient, and his mind was really on what Russell was doing. Which was zilch. Russell was behaving like you'd expect from a bowler who couldn't bowl. Martyred.

After I started putting the ball down where it belonged (still getting gutter balls), Dev made a big show of saying he was going to tape me so I could examine my performance at home.

He was pretending to tape me, of course. "Maybe he isn't faking," I said when Dev came to show me for the twentieth time how to approach the dots on the floor, the ones that show where to place the ball.

"Maybe. It's just that I've had a hunch about this one from the beginning. Okay, this is what you should do—"

I actually got down five that time. And Bruno thought that the life of a private investigator was boring. "Did you see that?" I yelled as I turned. But Dev was ripping off his bowling shoes.

"Our man and his buddies just left. No time to get my shoes. Here—" He shoved a twenty-dollar bill at me. "This should pay for everything. Give my shoes to Bruno."

"Hey, wait!"

"Good luck with your paper." I was left standing there with a bowling ball rolling back toward me. Dan McGrew never runs after a suspect in his stocking feet. Never. Sometimes if he's awakened out of a sound sleep, he might jump out barefoot (while behind him, a woman clutches her negligee across her chest). But that's it.

Pam came up to me. "What's the matter, Elliot?"

"He left." My voice was high, like a little kid who's been abandoned in a supermarket. I lowered it. "He left. He said I should get his shoes."

"I guess he had to go, huh?"

I nodded. "I guess."

"Do you think he'll tell you how his investigation came out?"

I didn't know. "I think it's confidential."

"How about a soda before you go?" she suggested. "Bowling is thirsty work."

So was surveillance. I hadn't had anything to drink since the day before. All in all, I was very thirsty.

Pam managed to find a bag so I didn't have to go around holding Devlin's shoes. A gumshoe's shoes. It almost sounded funny, but I wasn't laughing.

She was taking her break, so I asked her if it was okay with the management if I bought her a Coke as well. She said it was as long as she took off the red-and-white jacket with the lane logo.

Underneath she was wearing a yellow blouse that looked soft. It was a nice color. I told her so and she seemed pleased.

That was when I spotted a familiar face. Someone I'd seen, first on film and then in person, was coming through the main lobby. Again. "What's wrong with this picture?" I said softly.

Pam turned. "What are you looking at?"

Not what—*who*. It was Russell, who should have been wearing a neck brace but wasn't. He was with his buddies,

31

the ones he'd been keeping score for. Walking free and easy, like anybody else. He was carrying a bowling ball in a zip bag. One guy who was sort of fat wasn't there. Another had taken his place. It was the guy in the black pickup. "Jeez." I started laughing. "Oh, Jeez."

Pam had turned back. "What?" She reached out and grabbed my arm. "Elliot, what's so funny?"

"I think I know what happened. All the time we were watching him, he's been watching us. Russell knows Dev is a detective."

"How could he? It's not like he has DETECTIVE tattooed on his forehead."

"Nothing else makes sense. He must have lured Dev out and lost him." I went back to the bowling lanes and crouched next to the counter so I could watch them without them seeing me. Russell and his friends were getting set up at the lanes. Having a great time. Yucking it up.

I didn't hear Pam come up behind me. "Maybe he's just going to keep score again."

Without thinking, I grabbed her and pulled her down next to me. "They'll see you!"

"Elliot!" She was struggling. "It's okay if they see me. I work here." Since her break was over, she was even wearing her Lucky Strike Lanes jacket.

"Oh, yeah. Right. Sorry." I released her, but she didn't move away. I felt like the red design from the carpeting was reflecting off my face.

"Excuse me." That was Tiffany, the other girl behind the counter. She was leaning over, watching us curiously. "What's happening?"

Pam straightened. "Those guys on lane six, the ones who went out and came back—"

Tiffany nodded. "A while ago they gave me a tip to

32

hold their lane for twenty minutes. Something about a joke they were playing on some guy."

Pam looked down at me. "You were right."

I looked up at her. My legs were beginning to cramp. "I don't suppose you have your camera here, have you?"

"In my locker." She grinned. "I never leave home without it. And I bought some fresh film on my way to work. Why? Do you want to borrow it?"

I grinned back at her. "You bet."

Pam took me in back to the room marked EMPLOYEES ONLY. "Aren't you afraid they might recognize you?" she asked as she gave me a few instructions on how to use her camera.

"All kids look alike, right?"

"To some people." She examined me critically. "They might recognize your clothing. Tell you what, I should be able to find a disguise for you."

I'd died and gone to heaven. Less than five hours as a detective, and I was already doing undercover work.

"Won't you get into trouble doing this?" I asked as I buttoned a red-and-white Lucky Strike Lanes jacket over my shirt. The name Phil was sewn over the pocket, but she'd already told me that Phil wasn't scheduled to work that day. Pam's camera hung on a strap, and the jacket was big enough so the camera could almost fit inside.

"This is my last day. The job doesn't pay very well and, anyway, I'm awfully busy with the school paper and Photography Club. But I don't want to cause the manager any grief. Mr. Landrowski has been nice to me." She looked uncomfortable. "Another thing about leaving here. Martin's sort of jealous. He thinks that some of these guys flirt. Well, they do, of course. But it doesn't mean anything."

So Martin Nugent was jealous. This was a revelation, since he gave everybody the idea that Pam was lucky to be seen with him.

"The workers in the refreshment area wear red visors." She found me one of those, too. Before she put it on, she put some mousse on my hair and combed it flat. "Cute," she said as she fit on the visor. "You look sort of punk."

I examined myself in the mirror on the wall. It figured that the first girl who thought I was cute would have a boyfriend.

"Do you need your glasses?" she asked.

"I'll be okay without them." My eyes aren't great, but it wasn't like I'd accidentally wander down a lane. "Do you think it's enough?"

"Right now your own mother wouldn't recognize you."

MOM DOESN'T RECOGNIZE OWN SON. I looked into the mirror again and thought of asking if I could wear the jacket and visor home. "I—I don't know how to—" I stammered.

"Just take really good care of my camera."

Russell was looking awfully pleased with himself. One thing for sure—he was a good bowler. Every time he made a strike, he'd do a little jig. I got some great shots. Pam came over once to ask how I was doing. She took a couple of pictures herself. If the one came out with Russell jumping in the air with both fists clenched, I'd say that Dev had the makings of a first-class scrapbook to take to his client.

"Dev will pay you for these," I said though I couldn't be sure. I'd already told her I'd reimburse her for the film. "He has to."

"It's okay," she said.

The odd thing was that once I put on that jacket and the visor, I became invisible. A guy in my English class came in, looked straight at me, and walked right past. There were a fair number of people moving around, and nobody seemed suspicious about the caméra. Maybe they thought it was a service of the Lucky Strike Lanes, or maybe they thought I was taking pictures for publicity purposes.

I had taken almost twenty pictures when I felt this big beefy hand on my shoulder. I froze. Then there was this deep, deep voice. "I've been looking for you."

Uh-oh.

I turned to find this guy in another Lucky Strike Lanes jacket except double-wide. He looked around forty, so I guessed he was the manager. He was carrying some newspapers. "Yes, Mr. Landrowski?"

"Lane twelve. The kiddies' birthday party. One of 'em sicked up his cake and ice cream. Take care of it, Phil." He was looking at me peculiarly. "Did you change your hairstyle?"

"Well—yeah."

"I guess that's how they're wearing it these days. Gets the girls, huh? Too late for me." He didn't have much hair left.

"Oh, I don't know." That seemed a safe response.

He laughed. "You must be bucking for a raise. Too bad we don't give them." I laughed, too. He went off shaking his head.

I went over to take a look at the mess at lane twelve

35

and wished I hadn't eaten so much of the nice picnic lunch Bruno's mom had prepared. (Dan McGrew only has to deal with blood.) The kid was crying over what he'd lost, and his mother was telling him to shut up. She was also trying to apologize to me over the racket. *No problem, ma'am. It's all in a day's work.*

After strategically spreading some newspapers, I headed toward the counter to ask Pam where they kept the mop and the paper towels.

"Lucky you. Well, we've all had to do it." She unlocked the custodian's closet, then gave me a bucket and mop. I asked, but the bowling lane didn't keep a gas mask for emergencies. Pam also took back the camera because I'd shot almost a full roll.

Anyway, I took care of the mess. I was just putting back the cleaning things when Pam slipped the film in my pocket. "I'd like to see them when they're developed," she said.

"You will. Honest." Was that a date? "Well, maybe I'd better take off now."

"Maybe you'd better," she said, "before someone realizes that you don't work here."

"Okay." I started backing away. "It's been—"

"—fun," she finished.

"Maybe we can do it again—" I stopped. "I guess not."

"Oh, you never know." She winked at me and took a carpet sweeper out into the lobby.

In the EMPLOYEES ONLY I took off the visor and jacket. But I left my hair as it was. Maybe I'd get a hoop earring. I remembered to take the bag with Dev's shoes, and my glasses. I also transferred the film into the pocket of my windbreaker.

When I came out into the lanes area, I saw that the kids from the birthday party had left. Russell and his buddies were packing up their gear and talking about heading over to a tavern. Apparently the loser—not Russell—had the honor of buying beer for the rest of them. Russell was arguing about whether he should wear his cervical collar. The others didn't think he should take chances in case *that detective guy* saw him, so he finally gave in.

Little did they know that there had been a second detective guy and that Russell had been captured in living black and white.

Pam had come back. "He's here again," she whispered to me as we walked through to the lobby. "Your detective. He phoned a little while ago to ask if you were still here. Tiffany took the call, so I didn't know about it until now. He's just parking in the lot."

Was this great timing or what? Our instincts were already coordinated.

But I didn't think it would be too great if Russell saw us together. "Hey, thanks for everything. I'll see you at—"

"*You're not Phil.*" That was Mr. Landrowski. He looked shocked, and he wasn't the only one.

Russell and his group had just come into the lobby. They stopped.

They were staring at me.

CHAPTER FOUR

"**No, I'm not Phil.** I'm Elliot." I didn't know what else to say.

The man from the black pickup was staring at me. He frowned.

"Well, you'll have to excuse me—" I mumbled.

"What were you doing wearing Phil's jacket?" Mr. Landrowski was blocking my way, and believe me, there was a lot of him to block my way with.

Pam spoke up. "He's Phil's cousin. Remember, Phil had to visit his sick grandmother. He told you on Wednesday."

"Oh, yeah." Mr. Landrowski put one hand on my shoulder. "Are you looking for a part-time job? We have great opportunities, especially if you like to bowl."

I wanted to tell him that I wouldn't work there if he paid me. However, four big guys carrying bowling balls were closing in on my flank. "Maybe we could go to your office so I can fill out an application."

"Great."

The four were trailing after us, but they stopped when they saw the EMPLOYEES ONLY sign.

There was a side exit that I'd noticed earlier. "Mr. Landrowski," I said when we were out of sight. "My parents have really been after me to improve my grades. I was so thrilled by your offer, I forgot. They said I absolutely can't take a job this term." I looked at my watch. "In fact, I have to go home right now and hit the books."

"Too bad."

I barely heard him as I launched myself out the door.

"Step on it!" I yelled as I got into Dev's car. "Peel rubber. They can't see us together."

He just sat there. I tried to shrink because Russell's friends would be heading toward their own cars. I noticed Dev was wearing a pair of old rainboots. *"Peel rubber?"* You could see that he was trying not to laugh. "Did you get that out of a thirties' movie? Who can't see us together? And what happened to your hair?"

I babbled that I had film showing Russell bowling.

"Son of a gun," he breathed. "All right, fasten your seat belt." He glanced over his shoulder. "I guess he'll be all right."

Next to the picnic basket on the backseat was a carrying case like people use for transporting pets. "Is that a dog?" I asked as we started forward. I picked up one of my notebooks from the floor and held it open over my face like I was reading.

"Cat." We were moving toward the exit. "You know, if those pictures look like anything—"

"They will." They had to. I wasn't aware that I was holding my breath until we were out of the parking lot.

"Did it ever occur to you that you could have been in

trouble back there?" Dev's tone had become severe. "What if they saw you taking their pictures?"

"I can bluff."

"Some people can see through bluffs. Or they don't care to listen." He fell silent. "You did okay."

I had done okay. I continued to hold the notebook up over my face, just in case. "What's the cat's name?"

"He was in a kennel at the vet's," he answered as if I had asked a different question. "I've been away a few days. Hey, you can come out now. We're clear." I closed the notebook slowly. "I wouldn't mind an ice cream cone. What about you?"

"Sure, Dev."

We went to a Dairy Queen and Dev paid for a couple of soft cones, the largest size. "Uh-oh," he said as we started back toward the car. A black pickup with a license plate beginning ABE was pulling up nearby. Dev's voice was level. "Do we have a coincidence, or do we have a problem?"

"That's one of the guys who was bowling with Russell."

The driver was glancing in our direction and talking on a CB radio. "Let's get into the car nice and easy," Dev said. "No point in anticipating trouble." I managed to belt up single-handed. In the rearview mirror I could see that the driver was now watching us openly. His smile was grim. Dev handed me his cone. "On the other hand, there's no point in being a sitting duck. Hold tight."

I guessed that he meant to hold on tight to the two ice cream cones because both of my hands were full. The black truck moved at the same time as we did. Maybe it was just a trick of the sun, but the driver's eyes seemed on fire. I hadn't prayed since I was a little kid. But right then I was praying. Swear to God.

"Shouldn't you be driving faster?" I asked after we'd gone a few blocks. A second pickup driven by another of Russell's pals had come out of a side street. Now we had two of them after us.

"I'm doing the speed limit," he replied.

The speed limit? I was choked. What did the speed limit have to do with being chased by big guys in trucks? When Dangerous Dan goes on high-speed elusive maneuvers, sometimes he has to head the wrong way on the freeway. Or maybe he drives on the sidewalk and sideswipes a fruit cart.

"Besides, my cat is in the back. I don't want him to get sick." As if on cue, the cat started going *mrrawwwwwrl.* The yowl of a Siamese cat is like nothing else in the world except maybe an E-flat clarinet. "It's okay, boy," Dev called. "We'll be home soon."

"They're getting closer!" These were not small guys.

"Calm down, Elliot. They're only after the film. What's the worst that can happen?"

Ice cream was running down my arms while I mentally listed the worst that could happen. Death. Dismemberment. Disembowelment. Disfigurement. Have you noticed that words that start with *dis-* and end with *-ment* are usually bad news? "They could get the film," I said at last.

"Now you're getting the picture. Hopefully they won't. How about taking care of your hands with those tissues on the dashboard?"

"Okay." The two cones had turned to vanilla goo. Balancing them took some doing. Bruno's mom had provided

42

a plastic bag for trash, but it was in back and I didn't want to unbuckle my seat belt.

Mrawwwwwwwwwwwrrrl.

"Made it!" Dev yelled. I turned in time to see that he had gone through a yellow light, which meant that the red should stop his followers. But the black pickup was still with us. "Damn. There's never a traffic cop around when you want one."

"You mean that if you saw a cop, you'd try to get a speeding ticket."

"No, I'd pull over and ask for assistance—well, maybe just for directions to your house. Where do you live, by the way?"

I gave him my address.

Traffic was beginning to slow and I could see several people turning off onto a side road. "There must be an accident up ahead," Dev said.

"Lots of cops at accidents," I said.

"Lots of chances to be forced to stop nowhere near a cop." He turned off, too.

I could see the guy in the black pickup talking on his CB again.

"Why don't you have a car radio?" I asked him.

"My cellular's in the shop visiting its third world buddies."

I almost asked him then. *Aren't you afraid?* But he was concentrating on his driving.

"Hang on!"

The last of the ice cream landed on my face and shirt as we made a fast left turn through a parking lot. Then we made another left at the other side, which put us on a street without much traffic. The black pickup stayed on our tail. Dev was whistling tunelessly under his breath. I was starting to feel queasy.

The turn had not made his cat any happier. "I'll make it up to you," he yelled. "A can of that fishy banquet stuff you like."

"Don't say that," I moaned.

"Don't say what?"

"Fishy—anything."

"Oh, hell." I thought he was talking about my being carsick. Then I saw them. The black pickup was at our side. In front of us was the green Jeep. The Jeep was slowing. This was when *Dangerous Dan McGrew* usually cuts to a commercial. "I guess it's time to stop." Dev's voice was calm. "Don't worry, Elliot."

We all pulled over to the side, which was next to an overpass and practically deserted.

The man from the black pickup got out and came up to us. I groaned and not just because I felt sick. He wore a black T-shirt with a Harley-Davidson emblem and a belt buckle that said BORN TO DIE. "Elliot, keep your hands flat and in sight," Dev instructed.

My hands were covered with bits of Kleenex, but I put them on the dashboard. "Is this okay?"

"He'll want to see that you're not carrying any weapons."

Harley leaned down to look into the car. "Why don't you both get out and stretch? We need to have a little talk." Another guy was coming up from the Jeep. This one had a beer gut, probably from drinking too much of the brand advertised on his T-shirt. Russell was just behind him. He was wearing his cervical collar, walking so slowly that he was practically shuffling.

"Get out slowly, Elliot," Dev said. "No heroics. No-body wants to get hurt."

"That's right," Harley said easily as we got out. He motioned for me to stand next to Dev. "Listen to the man. Now, I don't know about you two, but I still got work to do on my rig today. And Joe's missus wants him to finish up in their backyard." He jerked a thumb at the guy with the beer gut. "So how about handing over that film?" He frowned at me. "Lord, boy, you're a mess."

"He's not a real kid," Joe insisted. "He's like one of those young-looking cops you see on TV, like those high school narks."

"I don't look young. I *am* young." I was hoping to be allowed to get older. "I'm fifteen."

Harley turned to Dev. "How come you sent out a boy to do a man's work?"

"I'm doing a school project," I said. "For life skills. We have to write this paper on future careers—"

"Elliot," Dev said through clenched teeth, "they don't care."

"Sure I do." Harley scratched his chin. "This kind of work—is it steady?"

"It pays the bills. Hours are lousy, though."

"No chance of going union, I guess."

"I'm the boss."

"Well, that's got its points, too."

"Hey!" That was Russell. "How about the film?"

"You'll get it." Dev straightened. "How did you spot me?"

Russell touched his collar. "A neighbor of mine works in a law office downtown. She recognized you when you came prowling around the neighborhood with your camera."

Mrawwwwwwwwwwwrl. "I have a sick cat on board," Dev said. "Come on, Elliot. Give them the film and let's get out of here."

I hesitated. "Wait a minute. He shouldn't get away—"

"Elliot—"

"No kidding. He's faking—"

"Come on, Elliot," Joe mimicked in a high voice. "Give them the film—"

Mrawwwwwwwwwwwwwwwwwrl.

I couldn't think of a way to stop them, so I reached slowly into my right pocket. It was empty.

I clawed through a torn place in the lining, but all I could find was a smooth rock that I'd picked up a month before. It had looked more interesting when it was wet. "M-maybe it's in my other pocket," I stammered.

"Maybe you dropped it in the car," Russell suggested.

"Maybe he needs a little help in finding it," Joe said. I couldn't believe what happened next. I mean, this guy was actually going to hit me. His chin jutted forward, and his eyes went sort of cold and piggy. The muscles in his arm bulged as he made a fist.

Dev and Harley both stepped between us, almost colliding with each other. "You don't want to do that, Joe," Harley said.

"The kid's pulling your chain," Joe complained. "Let me hit him just once. To help him remember where he put the film."

"Young man." Russell had gone fatherly. "This is not your concern, now, is it?"

"No, sir."

But I didn't have the film. And I knew I hadn't left it in the Lucky Strike Lanes jacket. Or had I?

46

Mrawwwwwwwwwwwwwwwwwwwrl.

"She doesn't sound very happy," Harley observed.

"He," Dev said.

Mrawwwwwwwwwwwwwwwwwwwwrl.

"Sounds real miserable, in fact."

"Look, I won't even break his nose." Now Joe was pleading. He turned to Russell. "I'll get it for you, Daddy."

Daddy?

"I don't know how long I can hold back these three sons of mine." Russell nodded toward the green Jeep, where I could see the driver reading a comic book. "Junior over there has the meanest temper of the lot. If he gets bored and comes out—"

Mrawwwwwwwwwwwwwwwwwwwwrl.

"Elliot, if you have the film, give it to them."

"I don't know where—"

Russell nodded. "Give him a hint of what can happen to him."

Joe stepped forward. He went *whoompf* as Dev's fist sank into his belly. I watched in shock as he jackknifed over.

"Aw, jeez." That was Harley. I could see he was ready to join in, although his heart obviously wouldn't be in it. The door of the Jeep opened and Junior started easing out. He was twice as tall as Harley, twice as wide as Joe, and twice as ugly as Godzilla.

I scanned the gutter for something to use as a weapon. The only bottle I saw was a plastic returnable. Joe had straightened by then. He took aim at Dev and knocked him against the side of the car.

This was so unreal that I kept expecting my clock

47

radio to go off. Or maybe Dan McGrew would drive up. Anything.

Mrawwwwwwwwwwwwwwwwwwwwwwwwwwrl.

My right hand closed around the smooth rock. Maybe I could get in one good punch without breaking my hand.

There was a flurry of motion off to the side. I blinked. Everything went in slow motion as a wolf leaped out of nowhere. A wolf leaped at me. With all its teeth showing. If I wasn't already flattened against the car, I would have been knocked over.

Not a wolf, a gigantic German shepherd. The dog stood on its rear legs with its front paws on my shoulders and started licking my face like I was his last hope for supper. His breath was hot and in need of mouthwash, but I didn't think of that too much because I was preoccupied with his teeth.

This dog already knew that I was vanilla-coated. If he discovered I was made of meat, I was in deep trouble.

"Is that your dog?" Harley asked.

I had to turn away before I could answer. "You'd better believe it." My face felt slimy with dog slobber. Then the dog discovered my hands. "If you go away now, you'll be okay. But if Killer thinks I'm in danger, he'll rip your throat out." I took hold of the dog's collar with one hand while he bathed my other arm to the elbow.

The driver of the green Jeep had returned to his vehicle. "I'm not messing with no dog," Joe said. Dev was bleeding from a cut on his forehead, but otherwise he seemed in control again.

"Go on," I ordered loudly. "You'd better get out of here. I'm already having trouble holding him back."

The dog was poking into my jacket pocket, ripping out more of the lining. Sometimes I keep snacks in there and

I guess he was hoping. Then I saw something and sucked in my breath. Across the street an elderly lady was holding a dog leash.

"You'd better go now—"

"Yoo hoo!"

The dog withdrew his head. He was holding something between his teeth.

"Fluffy! Stay there, sweetheart. Mama's coming."

Fluffy dropped the film and sat.

Harley stepped down hard and the plastic shattered with a sickening crunch. He ground the exposed film into the sidewalk, then picked it up. "Maybe I'd better dispose of this. Don't want to be no litterbug."

Russell regarded me sadly. "You've got a good future ahead of you, kid. Obviously you're a very intelligent boy. Only you have to stop doing stupid things." He looked at Dev. "You tell him that, okay? No hard feelings."

"It's not right," I said.

Russell just shrugged, then he and his sons left. I felt like crying, only I'd used up the last of the tissues. Fluffy loped back to his mistress, who fastened his leash. She led him away, lecturing him about how inadvisable it was for him to walk alone. Apparently there are all sorts of bad people out on these mean streets.

"Come on, Elliot," Dev said. "It's okay. Sometimes these things happen." I got in the car. He reached in back and picked up a slice of Italian bread from the hamper, then held it against his forehead to blot off the blood. I guess all the napkins had been used.

"Are you all right?" I could see that he was going to have a good-size bruise at the side of his face.

"Nothing that won't mend." He belted up. By then the other cars had driven off. "I'll go back to the lanes later and see if anyone is willing to sign a statement. Look, Elliot, you did fine. But you shouldn't have tried to hide that film. Those guys were mostly bluff, but you might have gotten hurt."

"I wasn't hiding it." My voice rose. "I was scared spitless. It fell inside my jacket, that's all."

He didn't say anything for a minute. "Watson," he finally said. "My cat's name is Dr. Watson." Then he started the car.

"Maybe some of the other pictures will come out," I said.

He had been pulling out, but he stopped so abruptly that I would have gone through the windshield if I wasn't belted in. A mild protest came from the cat, but I think it knew the worst was over. "*What* other pictures?"

I explained about the three pictures I'd taken at the end of the roll that Pam shot at the pep rally. We'd agreed that there was no point in wasting them. "I don't know if they'll be any good. They were only practice shots."

Pam was still at the bowling alley when we got there. I spoke to her briefly, then she went back to get the film. Dev told her he'd pay to have them developed and courier the other photos to her. She seemed concerned as she handed over the film. "I need these pictures by Tuesday," she said. "They're for the school paper. No kidding."

I said I'd see to it, and Dev looked at me peculiarly.

When we got back to my house, Dev asked if he could use the phone. I was hoping that Mom was home so I could tell her what happened. Neither of my parents was around. The door to the computer room was closed, but I didn't think anything about that.

I was really reluctant to see the day end. I asked Dev

if he wanted some coffee or a Coke or anything. Water was fine with him, so I got out an ice cube tray while he went to the phone.

I was running water over the tray to loosen the ice when I thought I heard a door open. Then I heard footsteps, only they seemed too light for Dev. "Mom?"

Then a high-pitched scream that sounded like Aunt Sheila.

And Dev shouting, "Wait, lady—don't!"

She maced him.

CHAPTER FIVE

OF COURSE Aunt Sheila apologized after she found out who he was. I'm not sure that Dev could hear her at first because he was swearing nonstop. So she started defending herself to me. "How was I to know that he was your detective?"

The instructions on the spray can said to flush the afflicted area with cool water. We led him into the bathroom, where there's a hand-held shower attachment with a million settings. Fortunately, it was set at Gentle Rain rather than Scale Fish.

Since Dev couldn't see very well, we had to lean him over the tub. Aunt Sheila had water running onto his face even before we got him settled. Soon there was water all over the bathroom, a lot of which was dripping off Aunt Sheila and me. Dev was the wettest of us all, but not by much.

I tried to introduce them when he raised his head to check on whether his eyes felt normal. By then Aunt

Sheila was arranging towels on the floor to sop up the flood. I sat on the closed toilet lid holding a couple of our best guest towels for when Dev was ready.

"You did look like an intruder, you know," Sheila said to him in her calmest tone.

He shut off the water and grabbed a dry towel that I held out. "No doubt."

"I've never seen you before, and you're dressed like . . ." Her voice trailed off.

I already said how he was dressed. Jeans and a sweatshirt that was no longer clean. Also, he was wearing rubber boots, and his face was bruised from his fight with Joe. I thought she had a point.

He started to dry off his hair, his clothes clinging to his body. Aunt Sheila turned away to throw some soaking towels into the tub. I don't think she knew that her wet blouse was almost see-through.

Dev was scowling at her. "So the idea is to mace first and ask questions later. Great stuff."

She stiffened. "That *is* the idea behind Mace, you know. It's not too useful in a home situation without the element of surprise. I could hardly ask you to state your intentions." He didn't say a word. "For heaven's sake," she said hotly, "I could have had a gun."

"So could I!" They were glaring at each other. His eyes were red, like a bull who had missed his nap. They were about the same height, but I'll swear that either Dev was getting taller or Aunt Sheila was shrinking.

"Dev has a gun," I said. "Only he wasn't carrying it today because he wasn't expecting any problems."

Sheila looked like she was about to say something else, then like she changed her mind. Then she spoke anyway. "I still feel I made the right decision."

He just looked at her and shook his head.

Soon after that, Dev left. I offered him some dry clothes belonging to my dad. He turned them down because he was heading straight home with his cat. I figured that he didn't want to have to return them. After this, he wouldn't want to deal with me, or any member of my family, ever again.

His back was ramrod straight as he went out the door, but since his boots were full of water, he squooshed with every step.

"I hope you weren't too disappointed," Mom said when she came home. She'd announced as soon as she came through the door that we were going to Georgio's for dinner and I could choose the pizza.

"Disappointed?" At first I couldn't figure out what she was talking about. Later I figured out that when she came home and found me sagging in front of the TV, she figured I was depressed. Exhaustion never occurred to her.

I wished Dad were there so I could tell them together about everything that happened. But he was working on some big job that took an actuarial whiz. Apparently the actuarial business was really hopping because Dad had been missing a lot of dinners.

I waited until Aunt Sheila and Mom and I were at Georgio's. Then I told them almost everything that happened at the bowling alley. I left out the car chase and the fight. Neither Aunt Sheila nor I mentioned her macing Dev. Mom didn't say much. She didn't eat much, either. We ended up taking home leftovers in a box.

"Elliot?" That was Dad, early the next morning. He was standing outside my bedroom door, which was closed.

55

His voice was soft, probably so he wouldn't wake up Mom, who likes to sleep in. "Elliot, some girl's phoning. She says it's important."

I blinked out at my clock radio. Eight o'clock.

"Coming!" I got up and pulled on my jeans, which I had left conveniently on the floor next to my bed.

When I came downstairs, coffee was perking on the stove and Dad was sitting at the kitchen table leafing through the morning paper. He was dressed for going into the office on a weekend, meaning casual but not too casual in case a client came in. I went straight to the phone and got a dial tone. I turned back to Dad. "You said . . . some girl." I was still groggy.

"Her number's on the notepad next to the phone."

I stared at the name he'd written. "Why would Pam Culhane be phoning me?"

"Good question. Why don't you call her and find out?" Dad smiled. "You must be getting older if girls are calling you."

I started dialing. "She has a boyfriend. Pam's the girl from the bowling alley."

"Ah. The girl from the bowling alley." He made Pam sound like the Girl from Ipanema. You know, the one in the song.

Dad must have come in after I was asleep. Unless Mom told him what happened, he didn't know.

Pam picked up the phone on the first ring. "Elliot? I need those pictures. The ones from the pep rally. It's vital that I get them right now."

"Slow down," I told her. "From the beginning, okay?"

"I'm not supposed to say anything. I just need the pictures. Or the film. Mr. Farwell says he'll develop the film personally if I bring it over to his house."

Mr. Farwell teaches journalism and photography as well as being the advisor for the school paper. "What's going on?"

"Do you have Mr. McCray's home telephone number?" Pam's voice was impatient. "He's not listed and I don't know the name of his agency. I called Bruno's house, but nobody answered so maybe they're in church."

"Pam, he doesn't have the film anymore."

"What! Elliot, I trusted you—" Her voice was loud enough that Dad gave up any pretense of reading his paper.

I explained to Pam that Dev had dropped the film off at a place with one-day service. The guy at the outlet had said the pictures would be ready after two o'clock. I said I'd call Dev myself and see what he suggested, but not now. The truth was, now that I had a reason to call, I didn't want to take the chance of waking him up.

I couldn't figure out what was so important about pictures of the pep rally. Since I had Dad's attention, I told him what happened while I was out with Dev. I wanted to tell him everything, but I didn't because you never know about adults. Sometimes they understand a situation when you don't think they could in a million years. Other times they close up for no reason.

"That's great," Dad kept saying. He started to laugh. "That's really great."

Then Mom came in looking half asleep. I went to my room to put on more clothes because I was still just wearing my jeans. When I came back downstairs, Dad was saying, "Aw, Lillian, do you always have to rain on the kid's parade?"

So I was prepared when I came into the kitchen.

"Stan," she said to Dad, "go ahead." To me: "Your father and I have been talking."

Dad doesn't tend to stand up to Mom, but you can tell when he isn't really agreeing with her. "What you did yesterday," he started. "It was great."

"It was luck," Mom said flatly. "Like winning a lottery. The TV news often runs tapes taken by amateur photographers. That doesn't mean they have the necessary talent to become war correspondents."

"It also doesn't mean that they haven't." Dad swallowed the last of his coffee. "All right. Detective work is more than luck," he said to me. "It's a combination of—" He stopped and stared into his empty cup. Then he shook his head. "Lil, the boy is trying to find his place in the world. Just like you."

Mom drew in her breath sharply. "It's hardly the same. I don't walk around with my head in the clouds."

I'd only been taking life skills for a few weeks. Job choices had been a big topic in our house for months. Mom wanted to find year-round work instead of just preparing tax forms. She had enrolled in a women's center career-planning workshop, only she hadn't yet found anything she wanted to do.

That was as much as Dad would say. He was looking at his watch. He stood and dug out his keys. "Gotta go." He gave me a small smile on the way out. "This discussion can wait. Right?"

"Right, Dad," I said as the door closed behind him.

Mom stood there until Dad's car pulled out. She sighed. "I just don't want you to be disappointed, Elliot."

Before I went out yesterday, my mother figured I was going to be bored. Now I was underqualified.

She put her hand on my shoulder. "You do understand, don't you?"

I definitely understood. The first time might have been luck.

Now I had to prove myself.

"What I love about my work, Elliot, is all the miracles I am privileged to witness. The lame walk—nay, the lame *bowl*—on camera." It was just after two. Dev and I were at the film developer's. Pam was supposed to meet us there.

I was relieved to see that his eyes looked normal. All that was left from the day before was a bruise on his forehead.

Three photos of Mr. Russell were spread on the counter. Dev tapped one of Russell releasing the ball. "Such form. The guy moves like a ballet dancer."

"Then the pictures are okay?"

"They'll do just fine." He looked at me. "I owe you."

"You would have gotten a picture of him," I said.

He shook his head. "I hadn't clued in yet that Russell had spotted me. I would have had to remove myself from the file."

I was looking through the photos from the pep rally. Pam takes good sharp pictures. There were crowd shots, and shots of the cheerleaders, and the principal making her speech, and Coach Garvey making his speech, and the goat, but none of the band from any angle that you could make out the clarinet players.

"Your pictures are all right?" the shop owner asked.

"Great." Dev slid the photos of Russell across the counter. "I'd like another set of these."

Pam came in, breathing hard as if she'd been running.

She was wearing a green Lincoln High sweatshirt. As she stood there getting her breath, the INCOL kept rising and falling. At the same time, the L and N expanded and contracted. It was like having an eye test but a lot more riveting. "Martin was supposed to bring back my car. I had to bike—never mind."

"Are you going to tell me what's happening?" I asked as she quickly shuffled through the photos from the rally. Dev was just standing there, but I knew he was listening.

Pam sorted out four pictures, barely glancing at the others. One showed the Lincoln High mascot being led out, the next a cheerleader slipping a wreath over the goat's curved horns. Then there was the principal giving her talk with the goat grazing nearby. The last showed Linc munching on his garland.

Dev put his three pictures away. "When I went to Lincoln, Hamilton was our biggest rival. I guess they still are. Anyway, back then Hamilton had a mule as a mascot. I'll be darned if somebody didn't take that mule just before the big game." His question seemed almost casual. "Did something happen to your goat?"

Pam must have remembered that she was talking to a real detective. We were alone in the shop, but she still looked both ways before lowering her voice. "He's missing."

Dev turned away briefly, and I thought he was trying not to laugh. "I imagine you'll get him back eventually. Hamilton's mule turned up at the game wearing a blanket with Lincoln's colors. Just trotted right out there on the field."

Her eyes were wide. "You think that Hamilton has taken—"

"Hey, wait. That happened fifteen years ago."

"Well, they can't get away with it." Pam was practically quivering with indignation. Watching her, I started to feel quivery myself. "Mr. McCray, you're a detective. Do you think you could—"

Dev was shaking his head. "I don't do missing goats." He stared up at the ceiling. "I don't usually even do missing . . . kids."

A kid is a baby goat. "I don't think that's a bit funny," Pam said.

"Don't worry," someone said in my voice. "I'll find him."

Pam described the situation more fully before we left.

The goat was at the pep rally on Friday. (I already knew that—I was there.) After the rally, Linc was tied to a tree near the field, as usual. Supposedly he was there to inspire our players during practice. The real reason had to do with his owners, Paul and Sarah Horton. Paul Horton is the only pro football player Lincoln ever produced. He played in Chicago two years, then came back to take over his father's farm.

When school ended, the goat was still there. Some kids go around the field or cut across to go home. Also, a certain number of people hang around the practices— girlfriends, sometimes parents. Joggers run around the field or use the track. The cheerleaders were out practicing. A lot of cars were parked on that side.

By the time anyone realized that anything was wrong, most everybody had left. Then suddenly Sarah Horton was there to pick up the goat and there was no goat to pick up. And no rope.

Coach's assistant was there. Coach Garvey had left early to deliver a bunch of equipment. Everybody was ordered to fan out because by then the sun was going down. All they were thinking then was that either Linc hadn't been tied securely or somebody had untied him. If he'd wandered off, he might be hit by a car.

No goat.

The SPCA was called and the Wildlife people. One of the players called his father, who works in the police station. Sergeant Goldberg promised they'd keep an eye out for an escaped goat.

"Can you imagine the police putting themselves out to find a goat?" Pam sounded angry.

By that time Dev was openly looking at his watch. "Gotta go," he said. "C'mon, Elliot. I'll drop you off at your place."

"If it isn't out of your way," I said, "could you let me out at school?"

After a minute, he sighed. "All right."

"Elliot," Dev said after Pam had cycled away. "You can impress women enough with flowers and a decent bottle of wine—okay, at your age, pizza and a Coke."

"I'm not—"

"Candy isn't a good idea. Either they're on a diet or some health kick. What you just promised is above and beyond. There's also a good possibility you won't be able to deliver. Big promises don't get big results. Believe me."

"I'm doing this for me," I said.

"For the school, you mean. Sure. Just keep telling yourself that. You have, what, two weeks until the last game?"

"Twelve days. It's on November seventeenth." I didn't want to explain to him what I was doing. It wasn't for

Pam. Okay, it was partially for Pam, but not in the way he thought.

It was the way Mom looked at me when she thought I had an unrealistic goal. It was the way Dad expresses opinions and then backs down. As for Pam . . .

When she was asking Dev for help, she had an expression on her face like she was praying in a church. She was asking for assistance from someone who could give it to her. When I offered, her face changed. *You can certainly help if you want to.* Like I was a nice five-year-old and she didn't want to hurt my feelings.

"I'm going to find the goat," I said.

On the way to the school, Dev impressed on me the importance of the first twenty-four hours after a crime. After that time, clues get lost and people forget where they were. Alibis are coordinated. The goat had last been seen Friday afternoon. This was Sunday.

"A football field." He shook his head. "Well, good luck." Then he drove off.

Okay, I admit I was hoping that he'd come with me to look over the scene of the crime. Or maybe that Pam would. Dev was meeting a friend. Pam and Martin were going to a movie.

Boiled down, this meant that I had to walk around by myself looking for goat plop.

CHAPTER SIX

ANOTHER IMPORTANT THING Dev said is that the scene of a crime should remain uncontaminated. In this case, if there was any evidence, an entire football team had already run through it.

This is the scene of the crime: Lincoln High occupies two square blocks with the fields lying behind the main classroom section. The gym and shop classes occupy a separate building at the end of the far field. Linc was tied in that area, which has enough trees and bushes so he wasn't always visible. Narrow roads for deliveries and the maintenance staff go through the school grounds and around all the buildings. So it would have been easy for somebody to drive in and pick him up.

I walked around in circles for a while. I don't know what I hoped to find—maybe a trail of goat pellets that would lead me to where Linc was peacefully grazing, like Hansel and Gretel and the bread crumbs. In the general area of the tree where Linc had been tied, I found some goat plop that looked like someone had stepped in it, but I didn't see any more.

After a while I went home. Mom was composing a letter on the computer when I came in. At first I just stood there.

Finally she noticed me. "Is there something you want, Elliot?"

"A goat," I said.

"Try the one that's hanging in the hall closet," she said. "You know, the one I bought on sale last spring. You've been growing so much that you should be able to wear it now."

If the goat fits, wear it.

"Not coat. Goat. Mom, where would you look for a goat?"

"Oh, Elliot, I never even made it past knock-knock jokes. All right, I give up. Where?"

"Skip it," I said.

I went out and tried on the coat in the hallway closet. I guess I *had* been growing because it was only slightly too big.

"That looks very nice." Mom had come up behind me where I was frowning at myself in the hall mirror. She put her head close to mine. Last year we'd been the same height. Now I was taller. "I don't remember giving you permission to get bigger."

She said the same thing when I started kindergarten. My reply was the same. "I have to grow."

She turned me a little so she could adjust the collar. "You'll get older and you'll leave home. And what will become of me?" Her eyes got shiny, and for a second I thought she was going to cry.

"Mom—"

"It's okay." She backed away. "Mothers are allowed to get weepy sometimes." Before I could say anything, she went back into the computer room and closed the door.

On Monday I decided to go to school early to talk to Coach Garvey. Pam had said that by the time anybody had noticed the goat was missing, Coach had already left to deliver a load of equipment in his truck. I still thought he might have heard something.

Coach has a tiny office off the gym, just big enough to hold him and a desk and a bookshelf and another chair. There's an upside-down horseshoe over the door, but otherwise every inch of wall is covered with framed award citations and photographs of players he'd taught.

The dates of the awards were pretty old. Lincoln High hadn't had a winning team in years.

On his desk was a photograph of his wife and three children, everybody with big smiles. His son is on Lincoln's second team. His older daughter, Melissa, is one of the cheerleaders who was practicing at the scene of the crime, so I wanted to question her as well. Melissa probably got her long dark hair from her mother, because Coach only has some light-colored fuzz on his head. However, he has a lot of wiry hair on his arms and legs.

Also on the desk were keys on a chain with a rabbit's foot. Coach Garvey was sitting in his chair, turned away toward the window. He was talking on the phone. "Mr. Calvin, I was telling the boys that I hoped we could count on you for a couple kegs of Calvinade. The boys sure look forward to drinking their Calvinade during the game. Oh, yeah, they're crazy about it. That's what gets them through." I saw him cover the receiver with his hand. "Hell," he muttered, "it's wet and it's got sugar." His hand lifted again. "It looks like we've got ourselves a winning team this year, did you know that?"

He wasn't exaggerating. Two years earlier, the school boundaries had been redrawn. We'd gotten some big guys who would otherwise have gone to Hamilton.

Finally he hung up after thanking Mr. Calvin five times and saying he'd send a boy around in his pickup to fetch the kegs of Calvinade (which tastes like Hawaiian Punch and isn't half bad). When he turned around, he was chuckling. He scooped up his keys, tossed them in the air, and caught them. Then he saw me and his smile faded. "What?"

"Coach Garvey—"

"You're looking at him." I could tell right away that he didn't recognize me with my clothes on. My regular clothes. Coach teaches some ordinary P.E. classes, including the one I'm in, but everybody knows his heart belongs to the football team. "Well, speak up, boy."

I swallowed. There's something intimidating about a man who can make you run in circles for an hour. "About the goat—"

He leaned forward, and automatically I took a step backward. "Sonny, I've talked to the principal about that goat, and I've talked to the Wildlife Society about that goat, and the pound, and I've given an interview to that girl from the school paper. Now, give me one good reason why I should talk to you. Otherwise I'm going to have to ask you to get out of my face."

"You've already talked to the school paper?" My voice was squeaking. "Was that Pam?"

He shrugged. "Maybe. Awful serious young girl. Nice blue eyes, though. Long hair the color of honey on a hot day."

"That sounds like Pam, all right." I moved toward the door. "Maybe I should talk to her first."

"Maybe you should." He started to dial his phone again.

I'd learned two things. The first was that Coach Garvey wasn't blind. The second was that I didn't have any right to ask questions. I wasn't from the police. I wasn't a reporter or technically even an interested party. Nobody had any reason to talk to me. I hadn't even gotten started, and already I was dead in the water.

If I'd realized that before, I could have slept an extra half hour.

Since it was still early, I decided to go to the school library.

"Sign our petition?" Outside the library doors a card table was set up in the hall under a banner declaring SAVE OUR PLANET. A senior girl was sitting there with her trig book open. In front of her were stacks of pamphlets about the ozone layer and porpoises, things like that. A clipboard held a petition with maybe twenty signatures. I read it. Something about not polluting the ocean.

"Sure, I'll sign." After returning her pen, I took a porpoise pamphlet. "Who do you give these petitions to when they're full?"

"God," she answered without blinking. "We figure that if we get enough signatures, She'll have to take notice."

That sounded more reasonable than handing them over to some oil company. "Well, good luck."

"There's a lecture tomorrow night," she said like she'd almost forgotten. "An environmentalist is giving a talk at the Unitarian Church at seven o'clock. He's reporting on his experiences in the Amazon rain forests. We're sending a delegation from our action group."

I'd tell Francie. "Have you heard anything about the school goat?" I asked.

She sniffed disdainfully. "We're only interested in endangered species."

I went into the library, but I came right out with an idea. The same girl asked me again if I wanted to sign her petition. She could probably reel off figures about polar ice caps, but she couldn't remember the face of someone who had been with her five minutes before. "Sorry," I called. "I'm in a hurry."

"He's in too much of a hurry to save our planet." Since no one else was anywhere near, she had to be talking to God. Joan of Arc started that way, too.

I went into the journalism room, hoping that Pam was there. She was standing in front of a window at a table with the four photographs of the goat before her. "Linc hasn't shown up," she said when she saw me.

"Good." That sounded bad. "I mean, that must mean he's okay. If something had happened to him, they would have found his . . . body." *Body* sounds nicer than *corpse*. Less dead.

"I guess." The morning sun was shining on her shoulders. *Hair like honey on a hot day.* "Sometimes animals are injured and they crawl away somewhere private to die. I've already heard enough jokes about kidnapping to last my entire life. But Linc's not a kid, Elliot. He's fairly old for a goat."

"I went out yesterday to look for droppings." That caught her attention. *Nice blue eyes.* Right now her eyes were tragic as though a pet she loved had disappeared. "I

70

don't know how often they plop, but I didn't see anything except in the area where he was tied up."

"Do you think someone's taken him?"

"It would make sense. Hey, you know what I was just thinking?" She shook her head. "I think we should spearhead an action group." I liked the sound of *spearhead*.

Pam blinked. "What kind of action group?"

"Save Our Goat."

She thought about that for a moment. "The initials are all wrong," she said. "SOG. How about Find Our Goat?"

"FOG. Sounds good."

She took a step toward me. "It's a wonderful idea. But I don't see how I can head a committee and cover the story at the same time."

"No problem," I said as if I'd cut a vein if it would bring back the school mascot. "I'll do it." I took a step toward her. This whole goat thing was definitely bringing us closer.

Her eyes widened only inches in front of mine. "You're sure?"

I nodded. Abruptly she took a step backward. She picked up her notebook from the table. "You'll need an advisor. Mr. Farwell might do it, but he already has his hands full with the Journalism Club and the Photography Club."

"Actually," I said, "I was thinking of Coach Garvey."

I'd never cut class in my life, but now I was cutting first period. The final buzzer sounded as I ran all the way back to the gym. No Coach.

His schedule was posted on his office door. Outside again, I spotted him on the far field, walking around the outskirts with his whistle in his mouth while freshman boys ran back and forth, colliding with each other. Every now and then you could see a soccer ball. I took off at a run. By the time I reached him, I needed a lung transplant and my heart was trying to smash through my ribs. "Coach," I wheezed.

He barely glanced at me. The whistle dropped onto his chest. "Fan out! Play your positions!"

I explained as fast as I could that we were forming a committee to find the mascot. Now the ball was in his court. So to speak.

"Do I look like a man with time on his hands—especially now? Oh, sure, I know what those English teachers say. Just because I don't have a hundred fifty papers to correct each week, that means I'm not legitimate."

"I've never heard anyone say—"

"If they want to hold a popularity contest, you see how many kids will turn out each week to cheer for Byron or Shelley." He blew the whistle. "Jeremy, watch what you're doing! Nathan, move out!"

"We're pretty sure that Hamilton High is holding Linc." Coach stiffened. "That's why we need you as our advisor. This is something that directly concerns the team. And morale." Coach is big on morale.

His eyes remained on the field. "Do you know something you're not telling me?"

"Fifteen years ago Lincoln took Hamilton's mule."

"Know about that, do you? Then you know they got it back. I'll admit there were some injured feelings about that little escapade. Hamilton doesn't even keep a mule anymore. In fact, we're the only team with any kind of mascot and that's just because Paul Horton donated him. Seemed a lucky charm at the time." He paused to blow his whistle again and yell and wave his arms. "Fifteen years is a long time to plot vengeance, don't you think? Fifteen years ago, half the kids in this school weren't born."

"Maybe." There could be some kid's father or mother waiting for the right moment to strike back, obsessed. Or perhaps there was a Hamilton student who had been brought up with only one thing in mind—getting Lincoln's goat. "Maybe not."

"I happen to think that students are more mature these days. You're not looking at a bunch of spoiled little yuppies with time to burn. Many of these kids have jobs."

"We know you're busy. It's not like anything would be asked of you."

"I've heard that one before." He blew his whistle again, then started to walk onto the field. He paused and turned back. "Don't you belong somewhere?"

By the time I got to English, my name had gone in as a missing person. I went to the office between periods to explain that I'd been talking to Coach Garvey. One good thing about having a clean record is that sometimes you get the benefit of the doubt.

After my next class, I ran into Bruno in the hall. "Hey, how did the rest of the surveillance go?" he asked. "Did you stay awake?"

"I took pictures of the guy bowling," I said. "Then his sons followed the car to get the film, and we had to take evasive maneuvers. They had us cornered until this monster dog came along."

"Sure, Elliot." He told me he was going to see the army recruiter after school on Tuesday, so I said we'd get together after that to work on his paper.

I have history before lunch. Mr. Hardy was just handing back a quiz when a messenger came in. He barely glanced at the note. "Elliot, you're to report to the office directly after class."

I knew I'd get in trouble if I ever tried to cut.

Everybody turned around to look at me. Mr. Hardy put my test paper in my hand like a consolation prize. I'd gotten a B+. "A little more effort, and you'll have an A next time."

People get expelled for cutting, only that usually happens when you do it a lot. Or if you use the time to rob banks.

When I got to the office, the secretary didn't know why I was there. "Oh, yes," she said after she looked through her IN basket for the fifth time. "Coach Garvey wants to see you."

Coach was on the phone again when I arrived at his office. "Yeah, well, Harv, I don't believe these boys really think about life insurance yet. I agree—time sure does go fast after you get to be our age. Oh, I have my benefits through the school." He frowned. "I wasn't planning to drop dead tomorrow. If I do, Marsha's going to have to be consoled by the insurance I already have." He nodded toward me and held up two fingers, which I figured meant that he'd be with me in two minutes. "I'd like to help you, only the school district has to clear any advertising material before I can hand it out. Regulations. That's right."

At last he hung up and faced me. "That guy was full of wind when we were in school, and he hasn't changed." But Coach had, just since that morning. He had become all friendly. "Well, Elliot, it looks like you had a point. I got a call about an hour ago from the local radio station. It seems that somebody phoned them. Hamilton High has taken credit for stealing our goat."

"Really?" I couldn't believe that I'd actually guessed right.

"It was an anonymous call, of course."

"Of course," I echoed.

I didn't catch what else he said right after that, not until he unfolded himself from his desk and was opening the door for me. "I know this is your lunchtime. I just wanted to get ahold of you so you can get this committee of yours in gear right away."

When I left home that morning I'd been a detective. Now I was spearheading a school committee.

"Elliot?" Coach was still standing there. "I want you to know that my boys and I will be behind you every step of the way." It had to be my imagination, but his tone sounded almost threatening.

By the end of the hour, the notice was ready.

HAVE YOU SEEN THIS GOAT? The picture we decided to use was the one with Linc wearing his garland. Linc was described as male, Angora, white, approx. 4 feet high, 11 years old. Pam volunteered the phone in her brother's bedroom for the goat hot line. He had left for college in September and her parents hadn't disconnected his private line yet. Her brother also had an answering machine, and she was positive he wouldn't mind letting us use it.

It would have been great if the number had spelled out something like 555-GOAT, but it didn't. The notice read: CALL 555-TURF WITH INFORMATION—ALL SOURCES CONFIDENTIAL. Mr. Farwell vetoed a slightly different version suggested by the sports editor. Before running off copies, he decided to check with Coach in the teachers' coffee room. Students aren't allowed in, so I waited outside.

There was enough noise from students passing in the corridor so I couldn't hear them distinctly. Mr. Farwell was being apologetic. He didn't want to step on Coach's toes since Coach was the official advisor to FOG.

"Dan—" Coach's voice booms no matter where he is. "Dan, you go ahead and stomp all you want. If my tootsies start to get sore, I'll be sure and yell." He saw me hanging around near the doorway and gave me a thumbs-up gesture.

But that didn't get me out of running laps. Once P.E. started, I became just another sweaty body to be whipped into shape. I wanted to tell Coach that I'd run around in circles enough for one day. I needed energy for the sort of heavy-duty thinking involved in recovering the mascot. Somehow I didn't think he'd be impressed.

After I showered and dressed, I went to Coach's office to ask if I could question his players after school. He said I could ask questions as long as I didn't interfere with practice. The cheerleaders would be out as well. He'd tell Ms. Greenwood to expect me so she wouldn't accuse me of wanting to pick up her girls.

"Did you know that my daughter is a cheerleader?"

I knew. Coach always looks like he's ready to bust his buttons with pride when he talks about his family, only I've never seen him wearing anything with buttons.

"Are you planning to question Melissa?" he asked mildly. Too mildly. I should have picked up on that.

"Well, she was there."

"She wasn't there all the time," he said. "She had to

76

leave early. A dentist's appointment or some such. I don't know that she was around long enough to see anything."

"Then that's probably what she'll say."

He was tapping on his desktop. "I just don't want to hear anything about you giving my daughter the third degree." The third degree? Me? This was unreal. "You're to be polite and respectful to all those girls. If I hear you're not treating them like ladies—"

He wasn't able to finish his threat because the phone rang. He picked up the receiver and a pained expression crossed his face. "All right," he said, "put him on." He looked over at me. "Go on, get out of here. Go do what you have to." I could hear him even after I closed the door. "Now, hold on, John. I never said your school took the goat. The radio station said somebody called and claimed—John? John, you don't know that for sure. One of the kids from your school might have—John, believe me, I wish I'd never heard of that goat."

I drew up a list of questions. I planned to ask everybody the same thing. *When did you last see the goat? Where did you last see the goat? Who did you last see with the goat?* I showed the list to Bruno when I ran into him in the hall.

"So that's what detectives do. Talk to cheerleaders." He punched my shoulder again.

Hey, it's a tough job, but somebody's got to do it. I signed him up as a member of FOG and gave him a bunch of HAVE YOU SEEN THIS GOAT? notices to post. I also gave some to Francie, when I told her about the environmentalist's speech.

Lincoln High has four female cheerleaders as well as Graham Temple, who is going with one of the girls. He

77

always says he became involved because it was the easiest way to keep an eye on Ashley around all those football players.

"We were working out a new routine," he said when I asked him about Linc's whereabouts last Friday. "Sure, I saw the goat, but it's not like I was exactly paying attention to him. By the time anybody knew he was gone, it was almost dark."

Ashley said the same thing. "I hope you find him. As goats go, he's okay."

The cheerleaders often practice by themselves. Ms. Greenwood had left almost directly after school, so she was long gone when Linc disappeared. The other two girls weren't paying attention either. Everybody was sorry and everybody hoped the goat was all right.

I saved Melissa for last, maybe because I wanted to practice my questioning on the others.

Melissa seemed edgy. Incidentally, she is a very pretty girl. She's short—sorry, *petite*—with dark hair and eyes that sparkle like Coca-Cola. Her eyes weren't sparkling when I questioned her, however. Not that she looked at me often. She was paying more attention to the football players working out nearby.

I wrote Melissa's responses in the notebook that Dev said I should carry. She said she hadn't been watching Linc, although she was aware that he was out there.

"I understand you had to leave early," I said.

"That's right." She brushed her hair back from her eyes. "I left about three thirty."

"And you didn't see anyone near the goat?"

"I didn't notice anyone."

"But you're sure the goat was still there." I had established the time of Linc's disappearance as between four and four thirty.

"Not really."

I asked her where her car was parked, and she pointed toward the street. That meant she'd crossed the field. Logically she should have seen Linc on her way out. "You were in a hurry?" She shrugged. "Where were you going?"

Those dark eyes blazed. "Where I was going is absolutely none of your business."

I definitely did not want to offend Melissa and have her run to Daddy. I apologized. Later I wrote down: *Melissa says her whereabouts none of my business.*

Investigate.

CHAPTER SEVEN

PAM HAD AGREED to call Tuesday morning at seven thirty if any messages came through on the Goatline during the night—sooner if a really urgent message came through. We didn't discuss what *urgent* meant, except it was like *Pay us a million dollars or the goat gets it.*

"Mom," I said when I came down to breakfast. "What do you know about goats?"

She was leafing through her *Larousse Gastronomique,* which is a cookbook about four inches thick. She didn't answer for a minute, but finally she stopped leafing. "Male or female?"

"Male."

She frowned. "How old? Under four months?"

"More like eleven years." I put a slice of multigrain bread into the toaster.

" 'The flesh of the male goat is not really fit for food: it is tough and has a very unpleasant smell.' " I looked at her. She was reading about Linc from her *cookbook.* "Listen to this, Elliot. 'Goat is eaten particularly in Spain, in Italy and in the south of France, but for reasons which have nothing to do with gastronomy.'" She paused. "Apparently goat flesh becomes disgusting after the animal reaches puberty. So I definitely think we should pass on having goat. What do you think about rabbit? I'm in an experimental mood."

Great. My own mother wanted to eat Thumper. "When I'm not around, okay, Mom?"

She's getting better. She didn't throw the book at me.

There was a time when my mom used to make ordinary meals and nobody complained. Her kitchen experiments started at the same time that she began thinking of a career. Every recipe had been a disaster.

"Maybe it's time to try octopus again." Mom looked up. "You know, you've been looking awfully happy lately. Does this mean that school is going well?"

"School's going great." I had just decided that it might be better not to tell Mom and Dad what was happening until I had things more organized.

"And your homework?"

I'd done my English report early so I'd have breathing space. "Things couldn't be better."

Mom looked as if she was about to say something like *Remember, it's always brightest before it starts to get dark.* She didn't. "Well, good." I knew what she was going to say next. She said it. "I look forward to seeing your next report card."

The phone rang while I was buttering my toast. Mom headed toward the wall phone. "Who would be calling at—"

I looked at the kitchen clock: 7:15. Even though Mom

82

had a head start, I beat her to the phone. "It's probably for me."

"Elliot?" Pam sounded excited. I was going to say something like *Hi, what's happening?* except that she didn't stop for breath. "Turn on your radio right now. 99.6 FM." She hung up.

"Wrong number?" Mom asked. She had picked up my slice of toast and was nibbling on it.

I headed over to the kitchen radio. "A friend of mine says something is coming on." 99.6 is the local soft rock station that Hamilton High called to claim that they had Linc.

The announcer was talking about fire department regulations for backyard rubble, so I put another slice of bread into the toaster.

"That's not what you're waiting for, is it?" Mom asked.

"I don't think so."

In the morning the station has this announcer who is always laughing. He can be announcing a tornado and sound like it's the funniest joke in the world. This morning was no exception. "Further to Lincoln High's missing goat . . ."

"That's it." By then Mom and I were both watching the radio like it was a TV.

"Coach Weaver of Hamilton High has denied that his players had anything to do with the disappearance of the goat, whose name is . . ." Papers rattled near the microphone like gunshots.

"Linc," I said. Mom regarded me strangely.

"Lincoln High's missing goat is named—guess what?—Linc. An action committee has been set up to find the animal. Find Our Goat, or FOG. The student in charge of FOG is Elliot Armbuster."

"Arm*bruster*."

Mom was staring at me.

"This is a message to the perpetrator from all of us here at the station. If Armbuster lives up to his name at all, I'd give back that goat. This guy sounds like he could take on Arnold Schwarzenegger."

"Elliot?"

Maybe I'd change my name to Armbuster. *Elliot* doesn't sound like somebody who goes around busting arms.

But then, neither does *Arnold.*

"One more thing, folks. The Lincoln High Alumni Association is offering a reward for information leading to the safe return of the missing Linc. Two hundred dollars. Cash money. Do-re-mi. The number to call is 555-TURF. That's F as in Fred for all of you with dirty ears and minds. Okay, you've all seen the posters hanging around town. I want every teenager within range of my voice to play hookey today. Go find that goat." He chuckled. "By the way, kiddies, that's a joke. I don't want your teachers blaming Uncle Ed if their classrooms are empty."

My toast popped up. As I grabbed it, Mom turned off the radio. "I don't suppose you were planning to tell us about this."

I started buttering again. "I was about to, but you were talking about recipes."

She started laughing, so it was okay. "No wonder you looked so strange when I mentioned recipes for goat. Oh, dear."

"The game with Hamilton is next Friday. I have to get Linc back by then."

"And that girl who called?"

"She's—" I stopped. "How did you know that was a girl?"

"The look on your face," she said smugly.

I decided to call Pam back. Mom was still leafing through her cookbook and mumbling about marinade. "I heard Uncle Ed," I said on the phone. "I didn't even know Lincoln had an alumni association."

"Oh, sure. They give out scholarships and things. Martin's dad is on their awards committee." A worried note crept into her voice. "Should I have cleared it with you before calling the station?"

I'd almost forgotten that I was FOG's chief weatherman. "Maybe. But that's okay."

It was more than okay. I could practically smell the missing goat.

"What's your opinion about Lincoln's missing mascot?" That morning, TV-journalism students were taking opinions in the hall.

Remembering how Dev's investigation had gone down the toilet once he'd been spotted, I declined to be interviewed for Lincoln's weekly slot on the community channel. My face was anonymous, and I planned to keep it that way. So I held out my hand toward the camera and kept repeating, "No comment."

I felt like a politician.

"Pam's in the darkroom," a girl called when I came into the journalism room at noon.

She didn't say to wait, so I went in. And wished I hadn't.

Pam was there with Martin. They were kissing, both

of them bright red from the darkroom lights like they were Demon Lovers from Hell.

"Sorry," I mumbled, and did the kind of 180-degree turn we practice in band.

"Oh, Elliot," Pam exclaimed. "I'm glad you're here."

That made one of us. Maybe they hadn't been in a total clinch like he was shipping out to war, but what I saw wasn't a casual peck either. I swiveled back. They were standing apart. Martin was glowering down at me with his arms folded. He's maybe six foot two, maybe eight feet tall. Maybe ten.

"Take a look at this picture." She was standing in front of a tray with a photograph in it. A crowd scene—I could tell that much from where I was standing near the door.

I was afraid to move. Martin's expression said *I can eat three of you for breakfast.* "Well, come on," Pam said impatiently. "We want to get over to the cafeteria."

Our eyes were locked, Martin's and mine. I tried to make my expression reply to his expression. *This is official school business, so back off and don't be a total dork.* I was hoping that at the very least, I didn't look like I was cringing.

I moved closer to Pam. "Let's see what you have." She had blown up a section of a crowd shot showing students standing next to the bleachers. One face in particular stood out. "Ken Slater."

She nodded. "Ken Slater." She pointed at another blowup, of several students near the outskirts of the crowd while the principal was speaking on the outside podium. "I think that's him, too."

This picture wasn't as sharp, and the guy was turned partially away. "Hard to say."

86

"Yeah, well, Ken Slater." Martin looked bored. "So that's it, right?" He waited. "Right?"

Ken Slater plays tailback on Hamilton's team. He went to Lincoln for his first year of high, before the school boundaries were redrawn. Offhand I couldn't think of any reason why he'd be at Lincoln's pep rally. "He was a year ahead of me in junior high," Pam said. "He doesn't seem the type."

"What type is that?" I asked.

She folded her arms. "He has a reputation for being serious."

"So he seriously stole the goat," Martin said. "The goat is seriously gone, right?"

"Yes, but—" Pam bit her lip. "His parents aren't well off. He fixes bikes at Wheels, and that's after school, after football practice. I know he's saving up for college. He's applying for scholarships, that kind of thing. He wants to become a doctor."

Martin looked disgusted. "Okay, I've never heard the guy accused of being a barrel of laughs. But he's on the team. This is rah-rah stuff. It didn't take much time to scoop the mascot. And you don't have to maintain it like a car. All the goat needs is grass and water. I don't think anybody has to sit around holding his paw."

"Hoof," Pam and I said together. Martin was getting taller again. The Not-So-Jolly Red Giant.

"The *police* have been called," Pam pointed out. "I can't see Ken jeopardizing everything by getting in trouble with the law."

"I can." Martin laughed. "Well, it's a blast, right? Taking a school's mascot in full view of its entire team. From what I hear, over at Hamilton they're ready to hang a medal on the guy who did it. Why not Slater?"

I didn't like to agree with Martin, but part of my mind was saying *Hey, why not?* If my whole life was school and football and a job, and I couldn't spend my money because I was going to have to live on it later—maybe it would be out of character, but at some point I'd almost have to bust out. "Whoever did it would have to use a pickup or a van. Do you know what kind of car he drives?"

"Some kind of old Jeep," Martin said. Too conspicuous. "Hey, anybody can borrow a pickup. So what would it take to make a goat cooperate? A carrot? A tin can?"

Motive. Method. Opportunity. It was all there. "I think this calls for further investigation," I said to Martin.

He beamed at me like we were buddies. Pam looked confused.

There was a knock at the door. "Coming!" she called.

Martin clapped his hand to his forehead. "Pam, I told you to remind me to call the garage about my car."

Pam started to apologize like she was his secretary or something. "I have a lot on my mind."

"Yeah, yeah, the goat."

The darkroom was like Noah's ark. When I opened the door, two other students were waiting, male and female. They looked at the three of us peculiarly.

"Okay, Armbruster," Martin said to me when Pam had gone over to get her purse from her desk. "Find the goat. I want my woman back. Her full attention—if you know what I mean."

"I'll do what I can."

Martin went off to make his phone call. I waited until he was out of the room. I was doing what he said, but I didn't think he'd be too understanding. "Are you available to go out with me tonight?" I asked. Look, I had never in my life asked out a girl. I didn't realize until I said them that I had used the right words.

Pam swallowed. "Elliot, I'd love to go out with you, but I'm seeing Martin." She looked genuinely regretful, and my heart started doing something weird in my chest.

"Surveillance," I said slowly.

"Surveillance?" Her gasp ended on a little laugh. "Oh, I thought—"

"I want to wait outside Wheels and see where Ken Slater goes after work. I don't have a car. If we find anything—" If we found Linc, the *Sentinel*'s ace reporter would want to be on the spot.

"Surveillance." Her face brightened. "Oh. Then that's all right. Elliot?"

"What?"

"What do you wear to surveillance?"

"Something inconspicuous and warm. Keep your fluid intake down."

"I get it." This is how she knew positively that we weren't going out on a date. On a date you get to use the bathroom. "I'll tell Martin something plausible," she decided as we left the room. "I don't think he'd understand the truth."

I didn't think he'd understand the alphabet. I was whistling as I left the journalism room. For the second time in four days, I was going on surveillance. And let's face it, Pam was a lot prettier than Bruno or Dev. And we were sneaking behind her boyfriend's back. And he was a senior.

Things were definitely looking up.

Pam managed to find out that Ken Slater worked until six thirty repairing bikes and cleaning up—later, if there was more work. She picked me up at six. Both of us wore jeans and dark sweaters so we'd blend in with the night.

Wheels is located in a semibusiness area of town with no buildings taller than two stories. The only houses are older, and there are a few trees. All that was open was a corner store. Pam parked down the block from the store and a long way from the nearest lamp pole, meaning that we were sitting in shadow. She was on the street side, giving her the best view of Wheels. We had already spotted Ken's Jeep up the street, so after Pam cut the motor, we just sat there.

There had been some rain earlier that day and the occasional car lit up the street like a river was flowing through. As time passed, I became more and more conscious of Pam breathing next to me, slow and even. I had never in my entire life sat alone in a car with a girl at night. At last I unbuckled my seat belt. Pam unbuckled hers. Unbuckled, we both stared straight ahead. I had no idea what to say, so I didn't say anything. After a while I yawned.

"Don't let me keep you awake." Lola's voice was silky. "I'll let you know if there's any drama."

I grinned. For once I was having trouble keeping my mind on the job. This wasn't just any dame. Chemistry, biology, life skills . . . everything was combined in one sweet work of art. She was class all the way. The problem was that I was just a gumshoe and she was a junior. Algebra couldn't make this equation come out right.

Even though the car radio was off, I began to hear music playing, sweet and slow. The night was cold, but I was beginning to feel like the inside of the sedan was cook-

ing. "They're playing our song," I said to her. "How about
a dance?"

Her laugh rang out like a bell. "You're nuts."

"Come on," I said. I didn't have to ask twice. Both of
us got out into the inky night. As our hands met, stars
spilled out like sugar overhead. The girl sighed and our
cheeks touched in the glow of passing headlights. We
turned slowly.

"Sometimes you're so nice," she said, "and other times
it's like you crawled out of the woodwork."

"Lola—" I murmured.

The love song ceased abruptly as someone in a nearby
house turned off his stereo. "What did you say, Elliot?"
Pam asked from the seat next to me.

"I was just thinking about this girl in ninth grade," I
improvised quickly. I paused. "No, she probably wouldn't
know anything."

Pam didn't say anything for a few minutes. "I told
Martin I was studying tonight." She didn't sound too
happy about that. "I've never lied to him before."

"You don't think he'd be jealous of me."

"He's not jealous, Elliot. But we're going together,
and he likes me to be there for him." She stopped, then
slowly turned toward me. "Why shouldn't he be jealous of
you?"

I continued looking across the street at Wheels. "Why
should he be? The guy's a senior. He's six feet tall."

"Six foot two."

"He drives."

"Elliot, my mother is almost five years older than my
father."

"I bet they weren't in high school when they met." No

91

high school goes five years, so that seemed a reasonable assumption.

"They were in their thirties." She bit her lip. "As for Martin being six feet tall—"

"Six two."

"Height is not the true measure of a man."

Wow. "Girls like guys who are tall."

"A lot of girls do. A lot of girls just want a guy who's nice. Who'll care for her. Who'll make her feel . . . cherished."

Sitting in the dark makes you talk about things you wouldn't talk about otherwise. There's a sort of intimacy when you can't see each other's eyes. This is peculiar because sunglasses don't have that effect at all. In fact, sunglasses make you feel superior, like no one can see into your head. Being in the dark together is like you've been accepted for what you are.

"Does Martin . . . cherish you?"

"I think he does."

Too bad. Otherwise I was beginning to wonder if I might have a chance at taking his girl away from him. Not that I'd necessarily live through the experience. Then she asked the question I really wish she hadn't. "Have you ever had a girlfriend, Elliot?"

That's when I saw him. "There's Ken." I was never so glad to see anyone in my life.

He was locking up. The lights were still on at Wheels. I figured they were left on all night so in case a burglar came he wouldn't have to stumble around in the dark while he was selecting a mountain bike.

We expected Ken to walk down the street toward his car. That's what he was supposed to do. He didn't. He started to cross the street in our direction. The hair stood up on my arms. "He knows we're here."

"No, he doesn't. He's heading toward the store. But he knows my face. Quick, kiss me. No, I'd better kiss you. Just stay still."

I was sitting there and suddenly I had an armful of Pam. I wasn't prepared. One of her elbows dug into my chest and then she sort of flopped across me. I tried to put my arms around her, but one of them was pinned.

As for the kiss—I tasted more hair than girl. I smoothed her hair back with my free hand so we could try again. So it was better the second time. "It's okay," she said, pushing herself away. "He's gone into the store."

"He'll be coming back out again," I reminded her. "Maybe we'd better stay close."

"Oh—all right."

Even though the light was dim, when she raised up a little so I could get my arm out, I could see that her lipstick was smudged. I put both arms around her, and she relaxed against me.

It was nice. I felt like I was cherishing her.

"Is he coming out yet?"

I hadn't exactly forgotten about Ken, but it hadn't occurred to me that Pam couldn't see the street because she was locked up against me. "Not yet." Then I saw him coming out of the market with a paper bag full of groceries. "Ken Slater at six o'clock high."

Someone I couldn't see through Pam's hair called to Ken from Wheels. He turned and started back in that direction. I whispered my observation to Pam, who has nice ears.

I was about to tell her that Ken was finally going

93

toward his car when suddenly someone slapped the top of Pam's car. "Hey, Martin, how's it going?"

We sprang apart. I've never seen anyone look as shocked as Pam when a guy I recognized as a senior leaned down to peer at us through the window. "Man, where's that ten bucks you owe me?" He had been grinning. His grin faded. "Oops."

I was history.

CHAPTER EIGHT

"**H**I, **JEFF.**" Pam looked sick.

"Hi," I said. "This isn't—" I was about to say that this wasn't what it looked like.

"Uh-huh." His eyes were narrow, disapproving.

"We've got to go," Pam said. She looked toward me but not at me. "Seat belt, Elliot."

Jeff backed away. "Well, see you. Tell Martin—no, forget it."

We pulled out. "Shouldn't you have given him an explanation or something?" I asked.

"There wasn't any time." She was sniffing. "Hell. Damn."

"Crap," I offered, and she laughed. Only it wasn't really a laugh. "Do you think he'll say anything to Martin?"

"Do you?"

"I don't know him."

"Yes, but you're a guy. Do guys tell guys things like that?"

Sometimes guys even made up things like that. "Are they very good friends?"

"They know each other. Card-playing buddies. You know."

"Do girls tell each other things like that?"

She nodded. "I wouldn't—well, I might. It depends on the circumstances." She grabbed a tissue from a box on the dashboard and blotted her eyes. She was definitely sniffling now.

Slater turned right at the next light, so we turned right as well. He was heading toward a road leading to the highway, where the car dealerships are. This is an area of town with side streets that are semiresidential—that is, some people keep chickens or horses, and there are lots of trailers on small acreage. It was a very possible place to keep a goat.

"This is definitely going to get back to Martin," Pam said.

"He won't believe anything was happening. He knows that girls find me very resistible. Guys always know that about other guys. Hey, I have to go on surveillance with a woman before anybody's willing to kiss me." There, I'd said it.

She sighed deeply. "Elliot, if you're trying to make me feel better, it isn't working. But thanks, anyway."

"You're welcome." What else could I say?

The distance between our cars narrowed as Ken Slater slowed down. He turned onto a small street and pulled up at a small house next to a kitchen equipment outlet.

Pam was praying under her breath. "Linc, please be there. *Please*. I'll never ask for anything else again."

We went around the block and parked. Pam took her camera and a flashlight, and I took my flashlight.

"I hope that isn't a guard dog," Pam said when we heard barking.

"It's probably just somebody's pet." Next time I'd borrow Aunt Sheila's can of Mace.

We stayed close to the kitchen equipment place, which wasn't well lit. Ken's Jeep was under a dim streetlamp, which cast the strongest light in the area. I guessed he'd gone into the house. We were getting close enough to see the yard beyond an old wooden fence. "There seems to be a small barn," Pam said. "No, wait, it's a greenhouse. The tool shed—no, it's too small."

I heard voices. Both of us clicked off our flashlights and ducked into the shadow of the wall.

Somewhere nearby a girl was laughing. Then two girls were talking at the same time. Ken Slater came out of the house with one of them attached to his arm. The other girl stayed behind in the doorway; she called something about not forgetting homework.

The girl with Ken held a small bouquet of flowers like they sell at the market. I could only see her outline at first, but she looked familiar. Then the door closed.

The two of them kissed. Really kissed. Like they couldn't get close enough to each other. I heard Pam gasp.

Ken's girl had her arms around him, so the flowers were behind his back. They were beautiful, she was saying. He was wonderful. Something like that. I remembered what Dev had said about flowers.

Then Ken was saying that *she* was beautiful and he hadn't seen her all day. Did she get any studying done?

A light laugh. No, she and her friend kept talking about him.

He wanted to know what they were saying.

97

Never mind. She didn't want him to get a swollen head.

Anyway, they sort of kissed their way very slowly to the Jeep, and that was the first I was able to see her face clearly.

It was Melissa Garvey.

If we moved from where we were, they would see us. So we had front-row seats to the Ken Slater and Melissa Garvey show. They didn't go farther than some minor league fooling around that wouldn't even draw a PG-13 rating. But when you're watching, and it's really going on, and you realize that this is what they're like on a public street—it starts you wondering what happens when they're alone.

At least that's the direction my mind was heading in.

I was also very conscious of Pam breathing next to me.

We waited until the lovebirds drove away before we returned to Pam's car.

"I've never been so embarrassed in my life," Pam said when we were finally able to leave. "I feel so—I'm so— that was *private*. Elliot, promise me that you'll forget everything you saw."

"You know I'm not going to forget it." Could she?

"I mean, don't repeat it. This is absolutely nobody's business. This is like—"

"*West Side Story?*" Maybe Lincoln and Hamilton weren't rival gangs, but I thought I saw a similarity.

"No! This is an invasion of privacy."

I never stop when I'm ahead. "Isn't that what newspaper people do?"

"I'm planning to work for a respectable newspaper, not some sleazy tabloid. That was so embarrassing." She pulled out into the street. On the seat between us was the wadded-up tissue she'd been sniffling into earlier. "Elliot, promise."

I gave my word.

"Maybe they're in it together," I suggested after we'd been driving for a few minutes. Pam had gone quiet, which didn't seem a good sign.

"I don't want to talk about them anymore."

"I mean like maybe they took the goat together. Like maybe it's a conspiracy."

Her voice rose. "Did they look like they were discussing a goat?"

"That doesn't mean they didn't take Linc. You said yourself that it was a good location. We couldn't see what was in the yard."

"Why would Coach's daughter help a Hamilton High tailback steal Lincoln's mascot?" Then she answered her own question. "Love."

Love. As motives went, you couldn't beat it.

Pam thought. "We have to come back when it's light." Then she remembered. "Martin's going to find out."

"He trusts you, right?"

"Maybe."

"If you heard about him and some girl . . . you'd trust him, wouldn't you?"

She shook her head and reached for a fresh tissue. "But I'd listen to him. I'd hope for a really good explanation. Only Martin isn't the best listener in the world."

"Hey, what's the worst that can happen?"

She didn't answer for a moment. "He'll dump me and rip off your face."

I just thought I'd ask.

· · ·

When I got home I kept thinking about Ken Slater and Melissa Garvey. About standing there in the dark next to Pam while we watched them make out. Pam said she'd been embarrassed, but I had definitely been turned on.

Dad was home for a change. "How's the great goat hunt?" he asked when I came into the living room.

"No goat," I said.

"Not yet." Like he was sure the goat would show up at our door any minute. "You seem to have the situation well in hand."

What I wanted to have in hand was the goat. Before the game. And I wanted to be the one to parade him around the stadium while the crowd roared.

I decided to call Devlin McCray, who had said he might be able to advise me if I got stuck.

He picked up the phone on the second ring. "McCray."

That's how I'm going to answer the phone when I have my own. *Armbruster*.

"Dev? It's Elliot Armbruster. You know, Bruno's friend. We went out to the bowling—"

"Elliot." He sounded patient. "That was last weekend."

"Uh . . . well, you said I could call you. About the goat."

"Oh, right. The goat. I've seen the posters around town. How's that going?"

"I questioned some people who were there, and I've followed up some leads. And I examined the place Linc was tied for goat plop—I mean, for clues."

He started laughing. "Elliot, I spend a good part of my days sifting through excrement. Welcome to the club."

That made me feel a lot better. "We still haven't found him."

"You might not. A lack of results doesn't mean you aren't conducting a proper investigation. At least, that's what I keep trying to convince my clients. What do you have so far?"

I told him what I'd found out about the goat's disappearance. "You said that you went to Lincoln when they took Hamilton's mule. Did you happen to know the guys who took the mule?"

Slowly. "I knew them."

"How did they do it? And where did they hide the mule?"

"Elliot, it's not the same. The mule was being kept at a farm belonging to the parents of a Hamilton player. A Lincoln student whose parents kept horses loaned a trailer to another guy—well, he didn't exactly *lend* it to him, but you get the idea. They drove out and took the mule. He wasn't in the middle of a football field. Anyway, this happened, what, fifteen years ago? I graduated in— yeah, fifteen years ago."

"I was born that year."

There was a long pause. "I'm not sure I needed to hear that. Look, you wanted to know where the mule was kept. Somebody else had parents vacationing in Europe. They figured he was eighteen, old enough to be left on his own. And they had high hedges."

"So maybe Linc's in somebody's backyard."

"Based on my own experience, I'd suspect any Hamilton student with a high fence or thick hedges."

There was something else I wanted to ask. I was glad we were talking on the phone and not in person. "Dev, do you ever follow people?"

"You know I follow people."

"I mean, like men and women."

"I don't do matrimonial work, if that's what you mean."

"I mean, Pam and I were following this guy because we thought he might know something. Only he was meeting his girlfriend." I stumbled through an explanation. "They really liked each other. It was sort of . . ."

"Sort of what?"

"Pam was embarrassed. They were kissing and everything. I mean, not everything. But it was more than just kissing." Not much more, but more than I'd ever seen happening live.

"You really have been keeping busy, haven't you?"

"I'm not supposed to tell anybody about seeing them."

"Any reason you should?"

"Not unless there's a connection to Linc's disappearance."

"Knowledge is a hell of a responsibility." I heard what sounded like a pop tab. "You said she was embarrassed. What about you?"

"Not exactly. Not as much as Pam. Dev—when guys see something like that, do they usually get—"

He cut in. "Elliot, I think this is the sort of thing you should discuss with your father."

"My dad's never done surveillance."

"Jesus. Look, I'm not an expert. There are men and men, and there are women and women. Basically, I think that men are more visually oriented. Women are most likely to get turned on when there are emotions and the whole can of worms. That's my opinion, which you can take or leave alone."

"Dev—"

"*What*, Elliot?"

"Earlier, when we were waiting for this guy to come out of the place where he works, we were sitting in her car. Then he started walking in our direction. Pam thought he'd spot us, so we started kissing. So he wouldn't see her face."

Sometimes you can hear a person smiling over the phone. I had a feeling that Devlin McCray was grinning like a fool.

"Offhand," he said, "offhand, at this time I'd say you have a more rich and fulfilling love life than I have. Did your aunt recover, by the way?"

"Aunt Sheila?" I didn't get it. Dev was the one who had been maced.

"When I left your place, she was still looking fairly shocked."

"She's fine."

We hung up after that because there didn't seem much more to say. "Good luck with finding your goat," Dev said.

I'd need it.

CHAPTER NINE

ON **WEDNESDAY MORNING** before first period, I was in the hall near the library when Martin Nugent roared out my name. *"Armbruster!"*

Many heads turned in our direction as he approached, scowling. Twice as many eyes stared.

"Nugent," I said weakly. For all I knew, Jeff had headed directly for a phone booth to tell him about seeing me with Pam in her car.

"Armbruster." Now he was smiling, but his smile didn't reach his eyes. His lips were drawn back like a shark sighting an Easy Swim class.

"Nugent."

As he advanced toward me, traffic in the hall came to a dead halt. The girl with the SAVE OUR PLANET table began slipping rubber bands around her pamphlets.

He stopped so close to me that I could smell what he'd had for breakfast. Honey Nut Cheerios and cocoa. I felt like I was about to get cavities from his breath when he finally spoke. His voice was low. "What's this crap I hear about you and Pam?"

"Exaggerated," I said. "Circumstantial." Maybe those words were too big for him. "It didn't exactly happen that way."

"That's what she says. Pam thought I should hear it from her first. She said that last night you two were following Slater."

"We were. That's right."

"She said that she thought he might recognize you—"

"She thought he might recognize her," I corrected. "He doesn't know me."

His face came closer. "I'm trying to keep an open mind about this, Armbruster."

That couldn't be difficult since there wasn't much to keep the wind from whistling through his ears. "I appreciate that."

"She said she had to make it look like you two were kissing."

His lips drew back even farther and I felt sure he was going to lunge at my throat any minute. She had to make it *look like* we were kissing? "That's what Pam said?"

"You didn't really kiss my woman." He didn't sound so sure any more.

I drew myself up to my full five foot seven. "We were looking for the goat." I tried to make it sound like we were seeking the Holy Grail. I'd heard there were strict rules about King Arthur's knights not fooling around when they were on a mission.

He nodded slowly. "That's what she said. But you know what this means, don't you, Armbruster?"

I didn't know what this meant. Maybe he didn't want to look like a fool in front of his buddies, so he'd just

106

break off with Pam and not kill anybody. That sounded almost like a happy ending. I'd even let Pam cry on my shoulder if she wanted. "What does it mean?"

He took a deep breath. "It means that from now on, the three of us go everywhere together."

Great.

Life skills was the only class I had with Bruno. The first thing I noticed about him when I ran into him before class was that he seemed really happy. "I talked to that recruiter guy yesterday. I think he wanted to sign me up right then."

I sucked in my breath. "You didn't, did you?"

"Naw, he said I should get my high school diploma first if I can. I got some great stuff on tanks. Armored. I think I really like the idea of being in an armored division. Or I could build bridges, except that's too much like construction." He nodded like he'd come to a decision. "Armored."

"That's great," I said with all the enthusiasm I could muster.

"I'll show you the stuff I got for my paper. When can I come over to your place so we can work on it?"

"How about Friday? I'll have to ask my mom, but you can probably come for dinner if you want."

"Sounds good."

We walked into class. Francie was sitting at her desk with a dreamy expression. I figured that she had been moved by the environmentalist's speech and now she was picturing herself defending the trees. Bruno and I went over to her.

"How was the lecture last night?" I asked her.

"Wonderful." She drew the word out. "He was inspiring." Her face became pink. "I'm meeting him tonight—Jason."

So she was interviewing him privately for her paper. "Great going," I said. No kidding, Francie was getting braver by the minute. In a small way, I felt responsible.

Bruno cleared his throat. "So where are you meeting this guy?" I thought that his voice sounded deeper than usual.

She glanced up at him and then directly down at her book. "A coffeeshop." Bruno nodded and moved away, but I thought he looked uneasy about something.

Ms. Winston came in. "I've heard that you're trying out your abilities as a detective," she said to me as everybody took their seats. "How marvelous for you."

"Yes, Elliot," Lester mimicked behind me. "You're just too, too marvelous for words." The guys at the back joined in with gagging noises until Ms. Winston called the class to attention.

It would be a whole lot more marvelous if I found the goat.

Later that day Pam asked if I had any major clues that couldn't wait a day. She and Martin were going out alone after school. I got the message. It was time to soothe her boyfriend's hurt feelings.

I told her that I had to practice my clarinet, anyway.

Mom came up that evening and asked why I kept repeating the Funeral March, over and over. "It sounds peculiar on a clarinet, Elliot. Besides, I thought your team is supposed to win this year."

The team. Football.

Rah, humbug.

. . .

On Thursday, in the absence of any other clues, I thought we should check out the house where Ken Slater had met Melissa Garvey.

With Martin along, I had to ride in back. He kept one hand at the back of Pam's neck while she drove, fiddling with her hair or her ear. I wanted to speak with Pam privately, but I couldn't because Martin was sticking to her like a second skin. I kept hoping that she'd shed him, at least for a few minutes.

"That's the house," she said at last.

We parked in front. In daylight it was clear that this wasn't a place with a goat. True, there was a fenced yard that was maybe half an acre. But this was the home of a gardener. One of my aunts has a home like this. She thinks that the worst threat to mankind isn't the Greenhouse Effect or the Bomb or overpopulation. It's aphids. This type does not have a goat as a houseguest.

The three of us walked up to the house and rang the doorbell.

A woman answered, about my mother's age. She wore a man's shirt over jeans that were almost green at the knees. "I don't buy chocolate bars," she said when she saw us. "Nor magazines. And I don't want to hear you practice your sales pitch so you can win a trip to Europe." She started to close the door again.

"Excuse me." Pam has a very friendly, open smile. "We're from Lincoln High and we're not selling anything."

That relaxed her a little. "My daughter goes to Hamilton. She's a good friend of a girl who goes to Lincoln. Melissa Garvey."

"One of our cheerleaders," I said.

Pam nodded. "I know Melissa. She's really nice."

"Nice legs," Martin said. I don't think the woman heard him, but Pam obviously did. I could have added that Melissa also has a pretty good caboose. I didn't.

The woman touched her collar. "I have to get ready for an appointment. Could you state your business?"

I held up a copy of the HAVE YOU SEEN THIS GOAT? poster. "I'm in charge of the search for the missing school mascot."

She folded her arms. "Haven't you found that animal yet?"

"Well, no. This seems like an area where a goat could be kept."

The woman had a dry laugh. "Young man, I'm a Hamilton High mother. I don't know if I should even be talking to you. They're getting quite a few chuckles about this at the school, you know."

"They're laughing at Lincoln?" Martin looked dumbstruck, like the thought hadn't occurred to him before. "They're laughing at *us?*"

"Kinda gets your goat, doesn't it, young man?"

Pam and I laughed dutifully at that one even though we'd already heard it a thousand times.

"Linc isn't a very young goat," Pam said. "We're sure this is just a practical joke. But we're really concerned about him. We were wondering if you've seen anything."

"I haven't *seen* anything," the woman said slowly. "But you know—" She came out onto her porch and then started down the front walk. We followed. "All right, you go down all the way to the end of Julie Road. The name changes to Williams. Go down Williams to where it crosses Henshaw. There's a big white house with a cement fountain, only it's dry. House needs paint. Nice

110

yard, though. Beautiful rhododendron when it's that time of year."

"Wait a minute." Pam had taken a notebook from her purse and was writing quickly. She repeated the directions, and the woman nodded.

"Who lives there?" Martin asked.

"Mrs. Oroville. She's an elderly lady who takes in strays, but nobody is sure what she does with them. The last time I drove by, I may have seen a goat in one of the upstairs bedrooms."

"Huh?" Martin again. Pam had stopped writing.

"I suppose that might be your animal. Some people say that Mrs. Oroville is a witch." She turned toward the door. "If I was planning to go there, I'd watch my step." The woman's laugh was harsh. "No, I wouldn't. I wouldn't go anywhere near the place."

Pam gulped. Or maybe it was Martin. Maybe it was all three of us. I think we were all feeling dazed as we walked back to the car.

For the first time, I didn't resent Martin's presence. He was the first one to speak. "You're not really going to see the Wicked Witch of the West, are you?" I noticed that he said *you*.

Pam was checking her camera. "I think we should follow up any leads." Her voice was level, but I caught a tremble.

Martin settled back against the seat. His shoulders were shaking, and for a minute I thought he was more afraid than any of us. Then he started laughing. "And I thought this was going to be dull. *Witches*. Jeez, what an absolute and total blast!"

• • •

111

"I guess this is it," Pam said as we slowed before an old house that hadn't been painted for a long time. A few windows on the upper floor were covered with plastic sheeting. "No cracks about haunted houses, okay?"

Not me.

Strangely enough, the yard was well cared for. Under a weeping willow was the fountain the other woman had mentioned. It had a sort of gargoyle on top that would have had water spurting from its mouth if there had been water running.

Martin didn't look particularly happy. "And there's a witch inside that house?"

"For the record," Pam said, "real witches worship nature and natural forces." She paused. "I read an article in *People* magazine."

Since we didn't know whether Mrs. Oroville read *People*, we all hemmed and hawed awhile longer. Finally we went up a well-trimmed sidewalk to a big porch with peeling paint and loose boards. When Pam pushed the doorbell, I halfway expected to hear a huge gong.

As it turned out, I didn't hear anything and no one came.

"Maybe we should look around back," Pam suggested.

"Maybe not," Martin said uneasily. "My mom doesn't always answer the door, especially when she's alone."

I knew I had to get used to the idea of snooping around. "I think we should look around back."

"If you were a witch, would you call the police?" Pam asked.

No, I'd turn us all into frogs.

"Hey! What are you kids doing there?" An older man with a big paunch stood on the other side of the fence holding a rake.

112

I looked at Pam. She looked at Martin. He looked back at her, then at me. I was still looking at Pam, who finally glanced in my direction. We all shrugged at the same time.

"I don't suppose you've seen a goat?" I asked the man.

"Not exactly." He waved toward the white house. "But if you're looking for one, it's probably in there. With her. I don't guarantee that it's alive, though."

"Nobody's home," Martin said.

"She's home, all right. Seldom goes out. I saw her looking out at me just a while ago. Making these so-called magic signs. Putting a hex on me. By rights I ought to be twenty times dead by now."

"Nobody would have a goat in the house," I said.

"Mrs. Oroville would. Now, if you'll excuse me, I'm getting on with my raking." He left the fence but stayed close enough so he could see us while we were at that side of the house.

"We can try the doorbell again," I suggested.

"Let's look around first," Pam said. Martin started humming the theme from *The Twilight Zone* as we headed toward the backyard. Other than some broken-down lawn furniture, all we found were a few fruit trees. An apple tree was loaded with ripening fruit.

"You already took the cherries."

We all turned slowly. An old woman was standing on the back porch holding a black cat, which was switching its tail. She wore a stained black coat five sizes too big for her. A knitted gray toque was pulled down over her ears. Her voice was accusing. "You got them all, the sweet as well as the sour. If you've come back for the apples, they won't be ready for a few weeks yet. They're going to be wormy. If you eat my apples, the worms will take over your insides."

The Revenge of the Killer Granny Smiths.

We had all moved closer together. "I rang the doorbell," Pam said hesitantly. She was watching the black cat, which was definitely watching her. Its green eyes didn't blink.

"I didn't hear you."

"We're hunting for a goat," I said. "Maybe you've seen our posters." I paused. "The goat was stolen."

"Oh, dear." Her voice sounded like the wind sighing through the trees. "You children haven't seen my gray kitty, have you? I try to keep them in, but cats get so upset when they're not allowed to roam." Her voice lowered. "He's poisoning them."

"Who?" Pam asked.

"The devil. You were talking to him."

This was definitely not *Mister Rogers' Neighborhood.*

"That guy next door is the devil?" Martin kept a straight face.

She straightened. "The devil is where you find him. The devil is in all of us, but more so in some than in others."

"Do you have a goat?" I asked.

She put her head to one side, and I could see that the cat was becoming impatient. "I believe so. You'll have to come in. But you must promise not to let out any of my cats."

Pam and I both promised to be careful.

Martin hesitated. "I'm allergic to cats." He looked at Pam. "If I go into a place with cats, my eyes start itching. And my nose runs and the whole thing. It's gross."

"Is it okay if I go in alone with Pam?" I asked him.

He scowled. "Are you trying to be cute, Armbruster?"
Well, yes.

"Martin, I don't need your permission to go anywhere with anyone." Pam was starting to look truly cheesed.

Score two for me.

We tried to introduce ourselves to Mrs. Oroville as we headed toward the back door, even though she didn't seem to be listening except maybe to her cat. Which was maybe her familiar. I'm not clear on the difference between a familiar and a pet except one belongs to a witch.

Inside, the smell was overwhelming—old litter box to the fiftieth power. I tried not to gag as we went into the kitchen. "I'm sorry that it's a bit close in here," Mrs. Oroville apologized. "I have to keep them inside, you see. Because of the poison."

Both Pam and I had put our hands over our mouths and noses. We peered at each other over our respective knuckles.

In the corner of the kitchen was a cardboard box with a calico mother nursing her kittens. She looked up to check us out. Other cats were coming in as well, although the big black scooted away as soon as it was set down. Mrs. Oroville shooed a gray tabby down from the counter. "Now, Smokey, you know you don't belong up there."

She took off her coat and set it across a kitchen chair. A black kitten immediately jumped up to investigate her buttons. "Perhaps we should go into the other room. I don't get much company, you know."

Under the coat Mrs. Oroville wore a green velour jogging suit that had seen better days. The cats looked well fed. Mrs. Oroville, on the other hand, was thin. Really thin.

The furniture in the living room was the type my dad

says they don't make anymore. Heavy. Sturdy. Scratched up with the stuffing hanging out. There were more cats.

Mrs. Oroville owned lots of books and pictures, mostly landscapes or ships. On the mantel was a studio picture of a woman in her thirties. "My daughter, Noreen," she said. By then I was getting acclimated to the smell. Pam had already taken her hand from her face. "She lives in New York City. She's a fashion designer. It's very demanding. She isn't able to visit often."

I picked up a black kitten that might have been the same one from the kitchen. The living room was becoming dark, but I didn't feel it was polite to ask Mrs. Oroville to turn on the lights.

"For my last birthday Noreen wrote me a lovely letter. She arranged for the gardening service because I've been having trouble with my hands."

"That was nice of her," Pam said.

"They've done a lovely job of it, don't you think? And they even bring big bags of dry cat food for me so I don't have to pull my wire cart anymore. The food is sold at the same place as their gardening supplies, you see."

"Do you hear from your daughter very often?" I asked. I was beginning to wonder if the daughter was as weird as the mother. I mean, my focus definitely wouldn't be on my mother's rose bushes if she was that many flakes short of a snowball. It looked like Mrs. Oroville was starving herself to make sure that a bunch of cats ate right.

"My birthday. Christmas. Mother's Day—she sent me a beautiful card last time. Would you like to see it?" She reached into a desk drawer and brought out a card with the usual *To the World's Best Mother*. She sighed. "Noreen's so busy."

The card was inscribed inside. *Mom, hopefully I'll get*

*out there this summer before you go off on your annual
cruise. The new showings are driving me wild. Try to see*
Phantom of the Opera *when it hits your area again. It's
spectacle, of course, but grand.*

"Do you have any other children?" Pam asked. Mrs.
Oroville shook her head. "Any other relatives around
here?"

"I don't come from this area. Fred and I moved here
when we were first married. Away from everything." Her
expression became vague.

"How long has it been since you've seen your daughter?" I asked.

"Perhaps—three years?"

It was getting really dark and I thought I should call
Mom to say I might be late. "Is it okay if I use your phone
to call home?"

People always say *Sure, go ahead.* I picked up the
receiver before she could answer.

"I'm not sure whether it's working properly," Mrs.
Oroville said.

No dial tone. This was not a phone on which you were
going to reach out and touch someone. "I guess it's out of
order," I said.

Pam looked troubled.

"Look," I said, "I can see you don't have a goat in the
house."

"Actually," Mrs. Oroville said, "I believe that I have.
There are enough other creatures. You'll have to come
through here." We followed her into a wide hallway. She
paused before a closed door. "I can't let the cats in here.
It's his den, his inner sanctum. Until my husband died, *I*
wasn't even allowed in here—no women or other living

117

things. But I believe I've kept it well enough so that even he would approve."

Nothing could keep out the smell of cat, but other than that, this was a den like you'd expect Hemingway to have. Knotty pine paneling, guns in cases, a heavy desk. A leather couch and leather chairs. And at careful intervals along the walls, the heads of dead animals, their blind eyes staring outward.

One of them was a mountain goat.

"Above all worldly pleasures," Mrs. Oroville said, "my husband enjoyed killing things."

I started backing out into the hallway. "We're looking for a goat that's still alive. Thanks, anyway." I had already tried flipping on the hall lights at the living room end, but nothing happened. I tried again.

"There's no electricity," Pam whispered as we followed Mrs. Oroville back toward the living room.

"I'm sorry I can't offer you tea," she said. "But I haven't been to the shops today."

I felt something and looked down. The black kitten was playing with my shoelaces. I picked him up again and he started purring like a brass band. I could see now that he wasn't all black. There was a small patch of white on his chest shaped like a comma.

"Do you have a cat?" Mrs. Oroville asked. I shook my head. "Then perhaps you should. In fact, I believe you've just been claimed."

I thought there was a good chance my folks would let me keep him since we had never replaced our cat that had died two years before. When we got back to Pam's car, I didn't see Martin at first. He stood up from under the weeping willow. "Did you find the goat?"

"It wasn't the right one."

He chuckled. Then he saw the kitten in my arms. "Armbruster, get that thing away from me. You're not taking it in the car."

Pam scowled. "He can't walk home with a cat. It's just a little kitten, for heaven's sake."

Martin went back to the fountain—in a huff, I thought. He stood there for so long that I thought he was communing with the gargoyle. "Armbruster, come here for a minute, okay? Maybe leave your friend with Pam."

Pam's voice was sharp. "Martin, it will only take a few minutes to give Elliot a ride home. Surely even your allergies won't act up in that time."

"It's not that. This is guy stuff, okay?" Which I figured meant that he was about to extend to me an exclusive offer of future disembowelment. Not that he sounded very threatening right then. "No kidding, Elliot. Get over here."

Pam took the kitten. "Guy stuff."

I went over to Martin, keeping my distance at the same time. He nodded toward the empty fountain.

Then I saw, too. "Hell."

"Yeah."

"Well, *come on!*" Pam called impatiently. "What's so interesting in the fountain?"

I was the first to speak. "Nothing."

"Yeah," Martin said. "Nothing at all."

In the fountain was a gray cat, lying stiff and dead. Its mouth was drawn back behind its teeth as if it had died howling.

"Do you think the old lady killed it as part of some ritual?" Martin asked. He hadn't been inside Mrs. Oroville's house.

I was about to tell him that her reputation for witch-craft was exaggerated. Then Pam came toward us. We headed her off.

"Look," I said to her, "I have to take care of something. Do you have a large garbage bag in the car?"

"I think so. Why?" I told her. My feeling was that the old lady didn't need to come into her yard and see a dead pet, and that the body wasn't going to get any nicer.

Pam handed the black kitten back to me. "Honey," Martin said to her as she headed toward the fountain. "You don't want to look."

But Pam was already examining the body. "I don't see an injury. My mother has a friend who is a vet. We can take the cat to her."

"I think it's a little late for a veterinarian," Martin said. "This is more like pet cemetery time."

Pam headed back to her car. "The cause of death should be determined. Mrs. Oroville thinks someone is poisoning her animals." She opened her trunk, then took out a garbage bag and a pair of work gloves. "Maybe I'd better take care of this, Elliot. If there's a cat disease going around, you don't want to spread it to—"

The No-Name Cat. "Okay."

So much for being protective. While Pam handled the corpse, I stood back with my kitten and Martin stayed well out of the way of both of us. His eyes were starting to get puffy.

"I don't suppose this puts us any closer to finding the goat," he said to me. He was sniffing and his voice sounded hoarse.

Probably not.

CHAPTER
TEN

MARTIN'S VOICE began getting rougher and scratchier as soon as he was inside the car, which had a dead cat in the trunk and a live one in the backseat with me.

"That's it," he wheezed after we'd only gone a few blocks. "Let me out."

Pam pulled over to the side of the road. She and Martin both got out. The kitten was trying out my lap for comfort, turning around and around. I hoped Pam wouldn't spend too much time apologizing because it wasn't as if she had a sandbox in her backseat.

The windows were up so the kitten couldn't make a leap for freedom, and I wasn't able to hear what they said. But I thought Martin was forgiving Pam. They looked like they were about to hug when he gave a huge sneeze. I held on to the cat as Pam opened the door and grabbed her tissues.

We drove away, leaving Martin standing at the side of

the road with a box of Kleenex. I held up the kitten to make one paw wave bye-bye out the back window. Martin was glowering as if his allergies were my fault.

"Let's get you home," Pam said. Now she was sniffing and I wondered if she was allergic to cats, too. Her shoulders were slumped and the back of her head definitely didn't look happy.

"Have you two been going together long?"

"Since the summer. July."

That seemed a long time to me. "What do you usually do when you go out?"

"The usual things," she answered. "Swimming. Movies." She didn't sound very enthusiastic.

"Have you ever thought about breaking up with him?" I tried to make my question sound casual.

"Sometimes I think a lot about—that he might want to break up with me." Right then she sounded like a little kid.

I immediately tried to reassure her. "Hey, Martin's no fool. I mean, he's not a complete idiot. He's not going to want to break up with you, not in a million years."

"You're trying to make me feel better again."

"I—*yeeeeeeeeeah!*" Ten tiny needle-sharp claws entered my thigh as No-Name decided he had found a comfortable position.

"Elliot, what's wrong?" We were stopped at a light. Pam turned around. "Are you sick?" Then she saw me trying to unhook the cat from my leg and started laughing. "Oh, Elliot, I do like you. You make me laugh."

I didn't see how she could really like me if she laughed when I was in pain except that a few seconds later, I was laughing, too.

After Pam dropped me off at home, I found the old

litter box we'd used for Tiger. There was even a partial bag of kitty litter in the garage, so after I settled No-Name in the kitchen with a saucer of milk, I filled it. The problem was that I wasn't sure if this tiny kitten could scale the sides of the box without being roped to a Sherpa guide. After he lapped the milk for a few minutes, I sat on the floor. I put him inside the box and scraped around to give him the idea. He thought that was a lot of fun and jumped at my fingers.

I heard Mom's car drive into the garage. Maybe I'd lead up to the kitten gradually. "Hey, Mom," I called when she came into the kitchen. "Did you have a good day?"

"A day like every other." She started to put her grocery bag on the table. "Elliot, what are you doing—" She let go of the bag too soon. The sound of apples and tin cans hitting the table startled the kitten so he made a lunge over the side of the litter box. I managed to catch him and imprison him against my chest. I waited for it. "Elliot," Mom said, "that's a cat."

When you're five years old, you can get away with saying *He followed me home—he's so cute—can I keep him?* At eight your parents think having a pet will teach you responsibility. At fifteen they know better.

I decided to use a diversionary tactic. I told her about the cat lady instead.

"Oh, my," she said after I finished. She was taking things out of the refrigerator to start dinner. No-Name had plopped in the sandbox. He started cleaning himself. (I know this girl who kisses her cat on the mouth and then wonders why no one wants to kiss her.) Then he went off exploring, tail held high. "Her daughter certainly sounds as if she cares. But perhaps she's one of those people who cares for other people only from a distance."

"In her card she said something about her mother going off on a cruise. Maybe Mrs. Oroville has some money hidden away."

"Her daughter should know her own mother's spending habits." She started putting things back into the fridge. "All right, let's go."

I stared. "Go where?"

"Let's go see Mrs. Oroville. Elliot, this is a very cute kitten, but the plain truth is that you'll be starting college in a few years. When you go, who do you think will be left with the cat?" She started taking out the food that she'd replaced. "On the other hand, if you're right and there's no electricity, Mrs. Oroville probably goes to bed early. Tomorrow we'll go right after school. No, give me the address. Tomorrow I'll take the cat back myself."

"Aw, Mom."

"Please don't whine. I have a splitting headache from all those tests I took today at the women's center."

Which meant that she still hadn't decided what she wanted to be when she grew up. Which I gather is particularly tough when you're already there.

"In life skills, Ms. Winston says that the most important question is what you really want to be, not the tests."

"I want to be deliriously happy." She began pulling out pans. "Challenged. How about fulfilled? Surrounded by intelligent people and sparkling conversation. Oh, and let's not forget rich. Well, adequately remunerated. But that's hardly a job description, is it?"

"Mom—"

"If you have an answer, I'm all ears."

"About Mrs. Oroville," I said. "Her daughter's address

was on the envelope the Mother's Day card came in." I told her where the card was kept. Maybe it was none of my business, but I felt like somebody ought to be told about the old lady.

"More detective work, Elliot? All right, I'll look into the situation. Now go see what that animal is up to. And don't give it a name. There's no point."

Like something isn't yours if you haven't named it.

I rounded up the kitten and put him into the box I'd prepared next to the stove. He settled down right away. I ended up tossing and turning for a long time that night. I'd come to the conclusion that if Pam really liked Martin, I'd better not make things any more awkward for her than they already were.

I fell asleep feeling noble.

I woke up Friday morning still feeling noble, although sometime during the night a sense of loss had been added. Maybe you can't lose what you've never had, but you can sure feel like you have.

I'd almost forgotten about No-Name until he came out of Mom's room. Mom was making her bed when I looked in. (Dad was away at a conference.) "Yes, the cat slept with me," she said. "And no, that doesn't mean a thing. He's going back. Oh—and take him downstairs. He must have to go by now, if he hasn't already."

After breakfast, I said good-bye to No-Name and left for school. Mom said she'd close him into the kitchen and then come for him after her workshop.

In first period a note came from Coach Garvey saying that he wanted to see me right after class.

When I went to his office, he'd just come from his

P.E. 12 class. His sweatshirt was stained under both arms, and his face was red, as if he'd been shouting. "Armbruster, we have a small problem here. You wanted to be in charge. You've got it." He nodded toward his window. "Take a look."

Outside was a small grassy area near the concrete bicycle racks. Only today there were no bicycles. What we had were two goats tethered to the rings in the racks, nibbling at the hedges. "Two?"

"Two pickups came this morning driven by two boys. Both are claiming the reward. These boys are definitely not collecting."

"Neither of them?"

He hesitated before answering. "I don't believe either of these animals is the right one."

I guess he must have dealt with Linc a lot through the years because both looked like possibles to me.

"I phoned Paul Horton. He's coming by shortly. He told me that most goats around here have identification tags in their ears. Did you know that?" I shook my head. "Another thing—the school secretary is getting all kinds of crackpot calls. The principal is not happy."

"I didn't tell anybody to bring a goat here."

"Yes, but you also didn't tell them not to."

I could see his point. Lincoln High was in danger of ending up with its lawn full of goats, chewing on everything in sight.

"Elliot, as soon as Paul leaves, I'm going to have these animals carted off to a shelter so their owners can claim them. No more goats are coming to Lincoln High as the result of your campaign. Do I make myself clear?"

"I'll call the radio station. I'll tell them about the tags, too." But I couldn't guarantee that anyone would listen.

"Yeah, you do that." Coach's voice sounded tired. "One thing this mess has accomplished is that school spirit is up. I'm noticing more drive on the part of our players."

"Because Hamilton took our goat?" But I had noticed it, too, at least as far as the students were concerned. I'd figured that things were different because this year we had a shot at the championship. It's not like anybody says *Okay, let's do our best* or even *Let's go out there and win*. What people actually talk about is murdering those Hamilton slimeballs, slaughtering them, pulling them apart, grinding their faces into the dirt, making them howl for mercy.

"Anything that can bring up morale is good. Anything that takes morale down is bad." He sounded as if he was reminding himself of something. Then he focused on me again. "I understand you've been talking to a former student, Devlin McCray. He's a private investigator now?"

"That's right."

"That's amazing when you consider that fifteen years ago he was voted—well, never mind. He was here during my first year. Not one of your better team players. It seems to me that he'd know more about mules than goats."

"He said he thought he might know the people involved in stealing the mule." I stopped because I didn't know the statute of limitations for mule-rustling.

"Did he say that he might have engineered the whole thing? Driven the truck?"

"N-n-no."

"That's only conjecture on my part, of course. Right after the mule disappeared, a girlfriend of Devlin's started a special project in her sewing class. She put together a

127

mule-size blanket in the school colors. I'm told there was a startling similarity to the one the mule wore in the stadium the night of our game with Hamilton.

"These things tend to be viewed differently when you're the one with the other side's mascot. Then it's a harmless prank. Things have changed this time because our mascot is missing. So I guess it all depends on whose ox is being gored." He nodded in a way that meant I was supposed to leave. "If you see Mr. McCray, tell him that Coach is truly astounded. Those exact words."

"Astounded about what?"

"He'll understand."

Dangerous Dan McGrew uses snitches. Some of them sell information for money. Others trade for Dan's silence.

Near the end of lunchtime I located Melissa Garvey in the cafeteria, working on her homework. Most students had left and she was alone at her table. I sat down across from her. "Hi."

"Hi." Her expression was cool.

"Elliot Armbruster? Remember? The goat?"

"Oh, yes. How's that going?"

Apparently the increase in school spirit didn't extend to this particular cheerleader. "No goat so far."

"That's too bad." Strangely enough, she sounded like she meant it.

"We've been following up some leads." I looked around. "One of Hamilton's football players was seen here during the pep rally. Ken Slater." As I said his name, I focused on her face.

She didn't give anything away. "Was he?"

"We—I thought he might have something to do with

128

Linc's disappearance. On Tuesday I followed him after he got off work."

She marked the page she'd been reading and closed her book. Then she leaned forward. Her voice stayed low, but every word cut into me. "Did you get a jolt out of what you saw, you little creep?"

I plowed on with my rehearsed speech, but I couldn't stop the hot color from flooding into my face. "I don't know whether Ken has any information about Linc's whereabouts. If he's heard anything at his school, I'd appreciate—"

"Are you trying to blackmail me?"

"No!"

"But you expect Ken to inform on his friends."

This was supposed to be a trade. She was supposed to understand that. Dangerous Dan buys information more often than my mother picks up milk at the market. It's almost friendly.

"We don't need names, just the goat. Hey, I don't care if you're seeing a Hamilton player. I'm not going to tell anybody. But if Ken knows anything—" I saw her expression and stopped. Melissa had no way of knowing that I'd keep quiet about her and Ken.

Nobody had ever looked at me before with such a mixture of hatred and contempt. "Drop dead."

With that she rose slowly, gathered her books, and walked away. I just sat there.

Lester stopped next to me on his way out. "You look like you're going to puke, Armbruster. Tell me it wasn't the tamale pie."

Maybe I wasn't advanced enough to use a snitch. Maybe I never would be.

129

CHAPTER
ELEVEN

"**I BROUGHT THE STUFF** from the recruiting guy," Bruno said when he arrived at my house on Friday night. "Mostly it's about tanks and artillery. He gave me some pamphlets about career opportunities. I told him to stuff the career. I just want to go into the army."

"What about officer training?"

"Not me, man."

We were sitting in the living room. Mom had left a message on the answering machine saying she had been delayed. She offered a few suggestions about what Bruno and I could have for supper. The kitchen had been cleared of all reminders of No-Name, meaning that he'd been taken back, so I figured that something was happening with Mrs. Oroville. I hoped the old lady was all right.

Mom's last cooking experiment hadn't been a re-sounding success, so there was a lot left over. I told Bruno we could make sandwiches if he didn't care for Mom's goop, but he thought it was great. In fact, he inhaled the whole pot. I ended up giving him mine and having a peanut butter sandwich. More and more I was beginning to like this guy. Bruno was like the big dog I'd never had, the one I wanted to sic on the neighborhood bullies when I was small.

"So," I said. "What do you want to say in your paper?"

He had all these army pamphlets spread out before him on the coffee table. "Elliot, man, I'm not very good at this stuff."

"Say what you want. Remember, we're also supposed to write about the bad points."

"Bad points?"

"Sure. Like, detectives have to sit around a lot."

He picked up a pamphlet. "There's some sitting around in the army. Like when you're waiting for air strikes."

"Another bad point is that you could get injured."

"I could get killed. Big deal. Armbruster, you could get killed riding your bike."

"I'm pretty careful."

"You think I'm not planning to be careful?"

Actually, I'd never thought of it that way. This guy wasn't a hotshot who was going to stand up and flash the enemy. He was slow and plodding, but he wasn't stupid.

"So write that. We have ice cream, if you want some."

"What kind?"

"Chocolate."

After we cleaned out the chocolate ice cream, I suggested that we work directly on the computer.

"What games do you have?" he asked when we were in the doorway of the computer room.

I told him. He started salivating when I mentioned Death Star Warrior Gods, which my dad was given by his boss with the warning that the graphics were excellent but they were giving his eight-year-old son nightmares. I baby-sat the boss's son once, and he gave *me* nightmares. So far I hadn't tried it out. "Let's do the paper first. You never know when a call might come in on the Goatline."

I ended up sitting at the computer console, which was not exactly a surprise. "Don't they want you to know typing in the military?"

"I'm not getting in and sitting behind any keyboard. The action could be in a whole different country from where I was."

"What about women in the military?" I asked suddenly.

"What *about* them?"

"Ms. Winston would probably like it if you mention women."

"I didn't ask the recruiter about women. They're there. They do a lot of the same things guys do."

I typed it in.

Women in the army do a lot of the same things men do.

"Have you ever gone with an older girl?" I asked casually.

At first I didn't think he was going to answer. "Pam," he said.

"*What?*" I swiveled around so fast that I completed a full circle before I was able to stop.

"Jeez, Armbruster." He was grinning down at me. "I just figured out why you're in this whole goat business. You have the hots for old Pam."

"I don't have—no. Well, maybe. It's just that we've been together a lot lately." My words sounded feeble, even to me.

"Hey, no big deal."

It was a big deal to me. Also a big deal to me was whether I looked obvious. "Do you think she's serious about Martin?"

Bruno had spent years in the same grade with Pam. "Is there anything she's not serious about? So, yeah, she's serious about Martin. Now, as to whether he's serious about her—"

"Well?"

"Hard to say. My gut feeling is that he doesn't think she's a whole lot of laughs."

"What about the other stuff?"

"Other stuff?"

"You know. Other stuff. Like when they're alone."

"How should I know what happens when they're alone? Am I there?" He was giving me that squinty look that means somebody thinks you're a pervert.

Maybe I was. I kept thinking about Melissa Garvey and Ken Slater, who hadn't been able to keep their hands off each other. I wondered whether it was like that for all the other couples around school, but I didn't think so. When we were driving home, Pam had been really quiet. I figured it was because she was embarrassed. Now I wondered if she had been measuring herself and Martin against Melissa and Ken.

"About older girls." Bruno shrugged. "Look, I don't hang around with high school girls. Most of the women I know, I meet after work—you know, when I'm helping my uncle Dom put up a house or something. Nobody asks me for ID if I go out for a beer with the guys after we knock off." He folded his arms. I swear the guy looked bored while he was telling me this. "I didn't start with girls. I went straight to women, okay? You buy 'em a beer. They wanna, you wanna, no complications."

I think I was gawking at him. If I went into a bar, I'd be asked for my ID. I don't even like beer. "Where do you take them?" I couldn't imagine in a million years bringing a woman to the house when my parents might show up any minute. Motels cost a lot.

"These are grown women. They have their own places."

There are a lot of opportunities in the army. "How does that sound?"

"You're fifteen, right?"

I nodded.

"No hurry."

"How old were you?"

He frowned. "I'm mostly interested in tanks. Put that in."

Bruno is mostly- I started over. I'm mostly interested in tanks. "Less than fifteen?"

He sighed. "Armbruster, let's just write the report."

We worked on awhile longer. Maybe Bruno couldn't talk very well about what a military career meant to him, but he was eloquent on the subject of tanks and armaments. I had him look up the information he'd been given about the procedure for getting into the army, and that filled more space.

We stopped to fortify ourselves with the last of a carton of banana fudge ice cream from the bottom of the freezer. I noticed that Bruno seemed to have something on his mind. "Armbruster, have you ever been out on a date?"

I didn't think I looked that backward. In fact, I resented his question. "A couple of times." Maybe they'd been fix-ups with the visiting cousins of friends, but I'd gone and everything had turned out okay.

"What do you do on a date?" he asked.

"Huh?"

"In case I ever—you know."

"In case you ever what?"

"Go out with a girl. Ask a girl out. That kind of stuff."

What was this? First he'd been talking about picking up women in bars, and now he was practically blushing. "Uh—Bruno? I thought you said you'd gone beyond dates."

"The other, sure. I just never went out on a date before. So what do you do? No, first, how do you ask 'em—girls—so they'll go out with you?"

"You just ask them." At least, that was the way it worked in theory.

"What do you do if they won't?"

Kill yourself. Figure the girl is going to tell her friends and they'll all laugh at you when you pass by in the hall. "I don't know if there's much you can do. Find another girl."

"Yeah, well, I'm doing okay. Only someday I figure I might want to do it. Date. Just to see what the fuss is about."

I always figured that the fuss was about what he was already getting. Maybe I was wrong. "As for what you do on dates, you go places or hang out."

"Like with guys?" He sounded hopeful.

Even I knew it couldn't be that simple. "You find out what they like to do, movies or whatever. Maybe it's something you like to do. Then you do it together."

"Okay."

"You talk."

"To girls?" I could see that he was envisioning a

136

lineup of females stretching out to the horizon, each demanding witty repartee.

"Not *girls*. You only go with one at a time."

"So I should talk."

Actually, talking was the only part I felt confident about. "You can always listen to what she has to say. I hear girls complain that guys never listen. It's supposed to be a good idea to say you're nervous so she can put you at your ease." I read that somewhere.

"What am I nervous about if she's already said she'll go out with me? I mean, we're there, right?"

"You're nervous that you'll mess up and she'll think you're a jerk."

"Me? You're kidding."

This guy was worried about being turned down, but after that he had no fears. Something occurred to me. "Are you thinking about asking out a particular girl?"

"No!" Too quickly. "Only, see, there's the winter prom coming up. Don't you want to go to the prom?"

"I guess so." My mind reeled as I tried to picture Bruno at a prom. Would he wear a bow tie over his army fatigues? A cummerbund? "Let's get this paper finished."

We managed to fill up two more pages. Bruno was just getting wound up about preemptive strikes when the phone rang.

It was Pam. "Elliot, I just played back the calls on the Goatline. We may have a hot tip. The call was fairly long. I'll play it on my tape recorder and turn up the volume."

The caller sounded like a male high school student who either had a scarf over his face or a bad cold. He said that Linc was being kept at a farm north of town and gave the directions. The most important part was that the guys

137

holding him thought goat-seekers were getting close. Linc was being moved out at midnight.

"Anonymous?" I asked when Pam turned off the recording. "There's a reward. That doesn't make sense."

"Maybe he's afraid the others will come after him for informing. We'll probably hear from him later." She paused. "So what are we going to do now?"

"Um . . . Bruno's here. Maybe we should check it out."

"Check out what?" Bruno asked.

I told him about the recording. "What do you think?" he asked. His eyes had narrowed like Rambo when he's thinking about a mission or his dinner.

"It could be a joke."

"Could be."

"It could be the truth. We could call the police."

"The police are not going to chase out there for a goat." By now he was pacing. "We can do it. Us. You and me. Jeez, Armbruster, if I can't liberate a damned goat, I might as well pack it in."

I could have reminded him that Linc wasn't a political prisoner being held by a corrupt dictatorship. But I didn't because I knew where he was coming from. We were spreading our wings, expanding our horizons, and sailing straight on.

"We can take my uncle Dom's panel truck. Do you have any gear?"

"Gear?"

"Like camouflage gear." I shook my head. "That's okay. I have extra at home. Do you have hiking boots?"

I had hiking boots that were practically brand-new.

Pam was enthusiastic. "Great! When can you pick me up?"

I looked at Bruno. "When are we going to pick her up?"

"Does she have any camouflage gear?"

"Desert or jungle?" Pam asked sweetly.

"Jungle," I repeated after Bruno gave his instructions. For somebody who didn't want to be an officer, he was sure acting like one. "Tell her we'll pick her up at twenty hundred."

"We'll be by at eight."

"Elliot?" Pam sounded like she was having second thoughts. "This has to be the last time we go out like this. If Martin finds out—" She stopped. "The thing is, if the tip is for real, I can't miss out on the story."

"I can always tell you what happened. Not that it would be the same."

"It wouldn't be the same at all. Oh, I almost forgot. Did your mother tell you about the cat?"

"I haven't seen my mother. She got delayed somewhere."

"I called earlier to leave a message about the vet's report. Mrs. Oroville's cat was definitely poisoned."

We were just heading out the door when the phone rang again. I figured it was Pam.

Instead it was Francie. I could recognize that breathy voice anywhere. "Elliot?"

"Francie?"

"Hi."

"Uh—Francie, we were just on our way out."

"Oh, that's too bad. See, I'm getting married tonight, and I wanted to ask you to do a favor for me. But if you're busy—"

"Hold on. You sounded like you said you were getting married."

"Who's getting married?" Bruno was staring at me.

"Who's that?" Francie asked.

"Bruno," I said to Francie. "Francie," I said to Bruno.

"Francie's getting married?" Bruno looked incredulous.

"Francie, run that past me again. You're going to—"

"—get married. Tonight. To Jason Dumont."

"Who's Jason Dumont?"

"You introduced us." I was about to protest that I couldn't have introduced them when I didn't know who the guy was. "Well, you're the one who told me that he was going to be speaking at the church."

"You're talking about the environmentalist? The guy from the jungle?" I could hear traffic noises behind her. "Where are you?"

"In a phone booth. See, I had to bring Tupperware. You have a car, don't you? My suitcases are next to my garage, and I was wondering if you could bring them to Jason's apartment. It's not like I can exactly go home. Not that I'm sure my mom is there because she's getting ready for this big trial. But if she is, she'll wonder where I'm going."

Next to me Bruno was mouthing something that looked like *What the hell is going on?*

She started to reel off an address. I wrote it down on the pad next to the phone. "Francie, are you saying that you're marrying—tonight—a guy you met Tuesday?"

"Uh-huh."

Bruno went on the extension phone in the next room. Maybe I didn't know the laws about these things, but I thought there were blood tests and waiting periods unless

140

they were planning to go to a state with instant marriages. "Where are you getting married?"

"His apartment."

"His apartment. Tonight you're getting married at his apartment. You mean a minister is coming over, right?" She had to be underage.

"It's okay, Elliot. Really. Jason is an environmentalist."

"Who's going to marry you?"

"Jason explained it to me last night. Marriage ceremonies are different in different places. There's a tribe where the woman simply moves her cooking pots into the man's hut."

So she'd brought Tupperware. Brilliant. "Francie, I'm not sure that's legal around here."

"Jason says—"

"When exactly did Jason say all this?"

"Mm. Well, after his speech, I had this whole list of questions to ask. So we went out to a coffee place, and we talked and talked and—it got really late."

I closed my eyes. "Is that all? You just talked?"

"He did most of the talking. We got together on Wednesday night, too, so I could finish interviewing him for my paper. Last night he had to speak at a banquet, but he phoned me afterward. Anyway, do you think you could get my suitcases? I thought I had enough money for a cab, but I only have my bus pass."

I almost asked why this guy didn't pick her up. It was obvious. She didn't want him to show up at her house if her mother might be there to stop them.

"We'll be there," Bruno said into the phone.

"Oh, hi, Bruno," Francie said. "I hope I didn't interrupt anything."

"We've got a mission," Bruno said. "But that's okay. You're on the way." He hadn't even seen her address.

"Francie?"

"What, Elliot?"

"Don't start your honeymoon until we get there."

"I have to go, Elliot. My bus is coming."

"Francie—"

But she'd hung up.

Bruno adapted well to the new set of circumstances. He called Pam to advise her that we'd be by at 2020. Then we made up the following plan of action:

1. **Don Combat Attire.**
2. **Commandeer Vehicle.**
3. **Rescue Maiden. (Bruno just put down "Francie.")**
4. **Reconnoiter with Journalist.**
5. **Liberate Goat.**

No sweat.

Don Combat Attire

We were at Bruno's house. I was trying on his old fatigues, which I think are called fatigues because the people wearing them carry artillery and heavy packs so they're always tired. I wore them over my clothes because (a) it was cold outside and (b) Bruno and I weren't exactly the same size. "Does this look okay?" I asked.

In answer he slapped me on the back. "Sure, Armbruster. You're a natural." He didn't say a natural what.

I examined myself in the mirror. Not bad. I mean, you put on army gear—even baggy army gear—and it doesn't matter if your skin is bad and your self-confidence isn't always the best. You look like a man. Unless you're a woman, in which case you look like one of those. "Yeah," I repeated as I turned slowly to see what I looked like from the side. "I'm a natural."

Bruno threw a bunch of stuff into a duffel bag. No weapons that I could see. A length of rope, a green metal tube the size of a roll of nickels that he called a cam stick, stuff like that. He told his mother that we were going out for a while. She said okay.

Commandeer Vehicle

"Don't you have a key?" I asked. Bruno was hot-wiring his uncle's dented white panel truck, the one with MAROS CONSTRUCTION on the side. The one that was parked in his uncle's driveway.

"Don't need a key." The truck started magically. It wasn't like Bruno hadn't tried to ask. He'd knocked on the door, but there was no answer. "Hey, don't worry. Dom always says that I can borrow the truck anytime."

"Shouldn't you leave a note or something?"

"This won't take long. He won't even know it's gone."

Next on the list: **Rescue Maiden.**

CHAPTER
TWELVE

WE SWUNG BY Francie's house. Bruno got out and crept around the side of the garage. He was back right away.

"Maybe we should tell her mother," I suggested after he tossed three heavy-sounding suitcases into the back of the van.

"Nobody's home." He got back in and slammed the door. "It's up to us."

We didn't have any problem finding the apartment complex where the environmentalist lived. Bruno parked in a visitors' slot. I noticed that he wasn't making any move to take out Francie's luggage.

She'd told us the apartment number. I pressed the button next to a tab that read "J. Dumont/C. Patterson."

"Yes?" The voice sounded tinny.

I'm never sure how to talk into intercoms. "I have something for Francine Raines. Is she there?"

After a pause, a buzzer sounded indicating the lobby

door was open. Just in time because Bruno was examining the lock.

I don't know what I expected to find when I got upstairs. The guy who answered the door was at least thirty, with glasses and a beard. He just looked at me, then glanced at Bruno, who was hanging back in the hallway.

"Francine! A couple of kids are here to see you." He smiled at us like we were trick-or-treaters. "Come on in. We were just making supper. Are you on your way to a Reserves meeting?"

"Not tonight," I answered.

I saw the Tupperware on the floor next to the couch, in a large shopping bag. You don't cook in Tupperware except in a microwave, and I didn't think that counted for a lot in the Amazon jungle.

Francie came out of the kitchen holding a wineglass. For a bride, she didn't look awfully happy. Her freckles were more prominent than usual in her pale face. If you ask me, what she looked like was scared. She set down her glass on the dining-room table. "Oh, hi."

He put a hand on her shoulder. "Aren't you going to introduce us?"

She wiped her hands on her slacks. She was wearing a plum-colored shirt that might have been silk and a gold necklace. Where her collar fell forward, I got a peek of something lacy under the shirt in the same purple. She was wearing makeup, too, so her eyelids were silvery. She was actually looking fairly sexy except that she wasn't smiling. "Well, this is Elliot. And this is Bruno. They're in one of my classes."

He nodded. "At the college."

College? We'd been promoted.

"And?" the man prompted.

146

Clearly she'd forgotten about introducing him. "Oh. This is Jason. Jason Dumont. Dr. Dumont."

"Ph.D. in Earth Studies. I don't take out tonsils." He was the only one who laughed. He looked at me more closely. "You must be one of those whiz kids I'm always hearing about who gets through high school at an early age. How old are you, sixteen?"

"Fifteen."

"Ah, to be fifteen again." He gave Francie's shoulders a squeeze. "Right, honey?"

"What? Oh, right."

A timer went off in the kitchen. "Maybe I should go check the wine sauce. Hey, I'd ask you two to stay for supper, but there really isn't enough."

"That's okay," I said as he disappeared into the kitchen.

The three of us stood there alone.

"Are you nuts?" I yelped (very quietly). "This guy has a beard. This guy thinks you're a college student. He thinks we're all college students."

Bruno didn't say anything. He just stood there with his arms folded, assessing the terrain. Very cool. He wasn't looking at Francie at all.

"It's not like I lied." Francie seemed near tears. "I didn't tell him I went to college. I said I was in school. He assumed—" She stopped. "The beard—I like it." She stopped again. "Do you have my things? I'm sorry— would you care for a glass of wine?" Bruno's gaze shifted to meet hers. She looked away.

Anybody else seeing Francie would have placed her at her true age. She had developed some over the past year—I could see that now—but if this guy thought she was college age, he'd been living in the bush too long.

Jason came out of the kitchen wearing a striped apron and holding a steaming wooden spoon. "Things are coming along."

Bruno looked at his watch. "Jason—"

"Yes?"

"We're on a tight schedule here."

"Well, if you have to go—"

"Actually," I said, "we've come for Francie."

"You're kidding."

"Jason." Bruno's voice had gone very soft. "Jason, this is total crap. Francie's fifteen."

The spoon hit the floor. Jason gaped at her.

Francie was already taking her jacket from the hallway closet. "I'm sorry, Jason. I really truly think there's been some kind of misunderstanding."

"*Misunderstanding!* You said you were going to be nineteen."

"I am." She was putting on her jacket.

"*In what year?*" Above the beard, his face was getting red. "Do you know the kind of trouble you could have gotten me into?"

"I could have gotten into trouble, too, Jason." She was stumbling over her words. "Only I—liked—you, and I was willing—"

"Well, I'm not willing to throw everything away for some little groupie." He made a move like he was about to follow her. Bruno put out one hand and he stopped.

"Who's C. Patterson?" I asked.

"Cathy." He breathed the name. "My partner. My wife. She's on a lecture tour." He looked upward. "Thank God she won't hear about this. Cathy would definitely not understand."

When the smoke detector went off, Francie was just

148

standing there with her mouth open, only no words were coming out.

"I think your wine sauce is burning," I said helpfully.

The Tupperware was the last thing that Francie grabbed. In the jungle, that probably counted as an annulment.

The van had the usual configuration, two seats in front separated by the engine cover, and a bench seat behind that. The back was all open space. I shared the bench seat with Bruno's duffel bag so Francie could have the other front seat.

"Don't cry," Bruno ordered her as we pulled out of Jason's parking lot.

"Hey," I protested, "she gets to cry if she wants to." After what she'd been through, I thought she was justified.

"Not in my truck. My uncle says that women crying is bad luck." He was chewing the end of his thumb. "Or maybe he said that women crying is bad news."

"Still—"

"I'm not crying." Francie was staring straight ahead. "I'm mad, okay? I feel like I want to spit."

"If you're going to spit, open the window." Tough as nails, this guy.

"I'm not going to spit. Maybe I'll throw things. Later. Not in your precious truck."

"Typical redhead."

Typical redheads have one heck of a temper. This was the first evidence I'd seen that Francie had any temper at all. "Ease off her, okay?"

He just grunted. I couldn't figure out why Bruno was so cheesed off except maybe we weren't going to be hitting Pam's place by 2020. I checked my watch. We were right on schedule.

Francie had started sniffing but with her eyes wide like a little kid who thinks that will stop the tears from flowing.

"There's a roll of paper towels in back," Bruno said. "Your stuff is there, too."

"I am not crying." She brushed the back of her hand across her eyes. "Only that guy was such a jerk."

"Well," I said, "at least you discovered the truth in time."

"In time for what?"

Bruno was the first to say anything. "In time so you could miss Mother's Day." Which was pretty good for him.

"Oh." Sniff. *"That."*

That.

Francie's place was on the way to Pam's, so I figured we'd be dropping her off. "You know what I'm really going to do?" she said after a few minutes. "I have copies of every *Rambo* movie. I'm going to sit down with a carton of pecan fudge ice cream and watch them, one after the other. I want to see guys spattered in forests and jungles all over the world." I wasn't sure, but I thought Bruno stopped breathing. "I'm going to have bad dreams and break out. And I don't care. Why don't you two come over to my place? We can watch together."

"We can't," Bruno said.

"No, I didn't think you could." She stared out the window.

"We have something else on tonight," I said. "Honest."

Okay, this is when I began noticing something weird.

I was picking up a sort of current between Bruno and Francie. I'd never noticed Francie before as a girl. Only there's something about a girl who's been noticed by another guy. She becomes interesting automatically.

Bruno sighed. "You can come with us."

"Where?"

"To get the goat," I said. "Maybe. We're following up a tip that was phoned in. We were just going to pick up Pam."

"Pam Culhane?" Francie was silent for a minute. "She's on the school paper. You won't tell her about Jason, will you?"

"Who's Jason?" I asked.

"Never heard of the kid," Bruno said. "Hey, wait, you don't have the right clothes."

"You mean I should be dressed like you?" Francie shrugged. "No problem. I have everything I need in my suitcases."

Of course. She had been expecting to trek into the jungle. No wonder her suitcases were so heavy. She was probably packing mosquito netting and a dugout canoe. All I'd brought along was a flashlight and extra batteries.

I was beginning to think that everybody owned fatigues but me. Tomorrow I was heading into an army surplus store.

Reconnoiter with Journalist

We drew up in front of Pam's house. While I was inside, Francie must have gone into the back of the truck to change because she was wearing army greens when I came back.

She was lacing up her boots in the backseat, so calm

that you couldn't tell she'd been upset ten minutes before. Bruno sat in front looking restless.

"You look like a war correspondent," I told Pam, who had a camera bag slung over her shoulder. We were still standing outside the van.

That seemed to please her. "No kidding?"

No kidding. She looked really good in her camouflage gear.

"You're looking pretty macho yourself." She spotted Francie sitting in back. "I'll sit with her." I slid the side door open farther. "Hi."

"Oh, hi," Francie said. "You're Pam."

"This is Francie," I said.

Pam climbed in. "So," I heard her say as I shut the door, "you must be Bruno's girlfriend."

"No," Francie and Bruno said at the same time.

I got in front.

"Then you're with Elliot." Pam was frowning.

"Elliot doesn't have a girlfriend," Bruno said. "Francie's along for the ride, okay?"

Liberate Goat

"You know," Pam said after we'd gone a few miles and the houses began to get farther apart, "I was wondering. Does anybody really care about Linc? Even Coach Garvey is only interested in what the mascot means to morale. I care, but I'm mostly interested in getting the story for the paper. Elliot?"

"What?"

"What does Linc mean to you?"

"That's a little complicated." Actually, it was a lot complicated. I had something to prove to myself, that I could be a detective. Both Bruno and Dev McCray had spotted the other, more obvious, motive before I was ready to admit it to myself. I wanted to impress Pam. "I want to find the goat."

"Bruno?"

"I'm interested in career opportunities," he said in the same way I coached him before he met with the army recruiter. Then he guffawed. I started laughing, too. In the rearview mirror Pam was looking at us with a sad expression. I didn't think we'd be the first people who ever did the right thing for the wrong reasons.

I'd forgotten about Francie.

"Actually," she said, "I have a broken heart. That's why I'm here." She was beginning to sound whispery again.

Bruno and I looked at each other, then we both shook our heads. Although *we* weren't supposed to tell Pam about Jason Dumont, apparently Francie was allowed. So as the hardtop turned to gravel and the road began to get bumpy, she started describing him to Pam. In whispers.

"Look," Pam said when there was a pause. "There was this guy I met last summer. Let me tell you the number he tried to pull on me."

More whispers. Every now and then a titter and *Oh, no, you didn't* or an *Oh, no, he didn't* or *That's awful.* I couldn't make out what they were really saying or whether I knew any of these guys they were giggling about. So there we were, rolling along like a slightly demented SWAT team.

Bruno was scowling. "Do you think you could keep it down back there?" he called. "We're getting close. I want to be able to listen."

"Listen for what?" I asked.

153

"Anything." We hadn't passed another car for a long time. He turned off the lights. "Crickets. Frogs. There's something about this I don't like."

"What?" We were both speaking quietly. He'd slowed down so we were almost coasting.

"We've been on back roads for the last five miles. I don't come this way often, but I think this is a place we could have hit faster if we came direct."

"Maybe whoever gave us the directions didn't know that. Or maybe they're telling us a roundabout way so nobody can see us."

"I like to know the names of my friends. What's this place called again?"

"He said the Alexander farm."

"Yeah, well, we're at the back, so I guess there's not going to be a sign."

Now we could see the lights from a farmhouse ahead of us. An area the size of an average city lot was fenced off, and there was a sort of open shelter inside that. I couldn't see the animals because, first, it was almost black outside, and, second, there were a lot of trees and bushes.

Bruno pulled over to the side. "We'll walk the rest of the way." He reached for the duffel bag and took out the metal tube I'd noticed earlier. "This is a cam stick," he said. "*Cam* is for camouflage. It has dark green coloring on one side and lighter green on the other. You smear it on your face."

I took the stick after he finished. It was like we were taking part in a primitive ritual. When I handed the stick to the girls, Pam and Francie eyed it as if it were a fish that had been dead for three days.

"I have a mirror in my purse," Francie said.

They sat there darkening their faces. "This color is

very good for you," Pam said as they finished. "It sets off your eyes."

"It makes your hair more blond."

I looked back. I'd seen my mom in a mud pack. This wasn't as thick, but it was hardly beautifying. "Just kidding," Pam said.

I shifted my attention to Bruno. "You know," I simpered, "I think this color is really you."

"Shut up, Armbruster." Bruno was eyeing Francie. "Your hair gleams—sort of like copper wire." He reached into the bag and brought out a black toque. "You'd better put this on."

"What about me?" Pam asked.

"You, too." He leaned over to rummage in the glove compartment and came up with a navy-blue toque.

The last of the giggling died away as the girls poked their hair under the tight-fitting caps. "We've got to have a picture of this," Pam said. "Not for the newspaper— necessarily."

"After we get the goat. After we get away from here." Bruno opened his door. "I want everybody to be quiet and stay close to me. Carry flashlights, but try not to use them. If there's any reason to seek cover, I want you to squint so nobody can see the whites of your eyes. Keep your teeth covered, too."

Then came the weird part as we moved through the moonlight with nobody talking. The house was a long way off, but we stayed near the trees in case someone looked out and saw our shadows. Underfoot were lots of little twigs and small branches, mostly soft because it had been raining recently. We were getting closer to the barn when I stepped into some really thick mud. Maybe it wasn't mud. My boots were going to be totally disgusting to clean.

The anonymous caller had said Linc would be in a pen next to one holding female goats. The location couldn't have been much better because the barn blocked the pens from the sight of the people in the house. As we approached, several goats came to watch us through the fence. The solitary male stood his distance.

"Listen." Bruno had stopped.

I listened. "I don't hear anything."

"That's the problem. We should be hearing more than we are."

Okay, we'd freaked out the frogs and the crickets. The goats were making bleating noises among themselves.

I found where the gate swung open. "Be careful, Elliot," Pam said as I unhooked the latch.

Look, I'd seen Linc being petted by everybody at rallies. He was not a dangerous animal. Bruno had a rope in his bag and we figured on tying him up after we got him out of the pen. We would also check his ear tag.

I approached the male goat slowly. "Hey, guy. We're here to take you home." He moved several yards away, then stopped. "Did everybody treat you okay? Did you make friends here?"

I turned back toward Bruno, who was standing in the open gateway. "I think he's nervous."

"Elliot!" Pam yelled. "Run!"

I ran and then dodged through the opening, but the charging goat still clipped the back of my legs. I staggered and would have fallen except that Bruno hauled me through.

Pam slammed the gate. "Are you sure that's Linc?"

156

Somebody laughed. A guy. Only it wasn't Bruno because right then he and I were dancing. I straightened up.

"Everybody stay absolutely still," Bruno directed.

We were barely breathing as we stood there in the dark. A twig cracked somewhere nearby. Pam grabbed my arm. She nodded toward the barn. Bruno and Francie were staring in the same direction.

Five long dark shadows appeared from around the side. "Well," a male voice said, "it took you long enough to get here. Which one of you is Armbruster?"

"Elliot—" Pam's voice was trembling as the shadows fanned out around us. "I just remembered something. Hamilton's first name."

We'd been told we were going to the Alexander farm. Hamilton High had planned an ambush, and we'd walked right into it.

CHAPTER THIRTEEN

"**O**NE THING I have to say for Hamilton High," their spokesman said. "We definitely have prettier girls." He was walking around in a leisurely fashion, shining a flashlight in our faces, one by one.

I wasn't sure, but I thought his buddies were holding two-by-fours. Judging from this guy's breath, they'd killed off some packs of beer while they were waiting.

"Get that thing out of my face," Bruno growled when the light came to him. I was standing at his other side.

The light went down slightly. "This is definitely not Armbruster. From what I've heard, Armbruster is the class nerd. Hey, who else would devote his life to finding a goat?" The light moved suddenly and landed full in my face. "Is that you, nerd?"

I was so startled that I flailed out and knocked the light from his hand. I don't know what happened next except that there was a short struggle beside me. "Turn on a light," Bruno ordered. "Shine it on me. Not in my eyes."

Pam snapped on a flashlight, just in time because this guy's friends were coming to his aid. Bruno was holding him, one arm around his neck and the other twisting his arm behind his back. "Jeez, man!" he shrieked. "You're breaking my arm. Easy!"

Francie had turned on a light as well. Pam started moving around behind us. She put a stick of firewood in my hand like I was supposed to hit somebody with it. This was definitely unreal. She handed one to Francie, too. Pam readied the camera.

"Everybody stay just as you are," she directed our shadowed counterparts.

They threw up their hands as the flash went off. I think that one of them knocked himself on the head with his two-by-four. He started swearing while the guy next to him laughed nervously.

Bruno tightened his grip. "Watch your mouth. There are ladies present."

Pam looked as if she was about to protest, but she didn't. I thought Francie had gone into shock. If nothing else, this was taking her mind off her broken heart.

Both the laughing and swearing broke off abruptly. "Danny, are you okay?" one guy called. "What do you want us to do?"

"Get the hell out of here," Bruno said. "I'm keeping your pal as a souvenir until you're gone."

"Wait. Hold on." Danny sounded like he was in pain. "Could you ease up a little?"

Bruno didn't move. "That depends on what Elliot says. He's in charge. The nerd, remember?"

"You seem to be doing okay," I allowed graciously. "Continue as you are."

"I don't like being dragged out at night like this,"

Bruno said. "I don't like being jumped. How do you like it, nerd?"

"You have a point." Danny grimaced. "Look, this is about the goat."

"Keep talking," I said. Pam was taking more pictures. I hoped she was taking care with her flash. All we needed was for her to blind Bruno.

I wasn't expecting the next thing Danny said.

"We figured you had him. The goat."

"You thought *we* had him?" Bruno looked so startled that he loosened his grip slightly.

"Maybe not you. Somebody from your school. We figured it was Armbruster. If you hadn't shown up, we'd know it was you, right?"

"Excuse me," Pam said. "You're saying you lured us down here for a goat you say we already have. That doesn't make sense."

"We're getting a load of flak at school," another voice said. "Visits from the cops. Lectures from Coach Weaver. If we don't have the goat and nobody has turned it in for the reward, somebody from your school must have it."

"Nice touch," Danny said, "offering a reward for a goat that isn't really missing. Lots of publicity, no payoff."

"Face it, sleazeball," I said. "Somebody at your school isn't interested in claiming the reward." Whoever this saint was, he'd probably claim the glory after the game.

I was paying so much attention to our captive and it was so dark outside the circle of light that I didn't notice that all four of the other guys were no longer there.

Suddenly the beam from Francie's flashlight was all over the place. "Gotcha, sweetheart," another guy said.

There was a struggle and a splat as a body hit the mud, hard. The flashlight rolled.

161

"Francie!" Bruno called. "Are you okay? Francie?"

"Oh, gosh," Francie said. "I'm—(grunt)—awfully sorry."

"Hold this guy," Bruno said, shoving Danny at me.

"Me?" Me. I menaced him with the club and hoped he wouldn't take it from me. I growled—swear to God.

Pam shone her flashlight in the direction of the grunts. I blinked. Francie had this guy who was at least six feet tall facedown in mud and manure. Her knee was planted in the middle of his back and she had one of his arms stretched behind him. "Oh, God," she said, "I hope I'm not hurting you."

Bruno took a second to react. "You're doing fine." He turned. "Elliot?"

"You're looking at raw nerd power." I raised the club again.

Danny kept rubbing the arm that Bruno had been twisting. He eyed me nervously. "Watch what you're doing with that thing."

"You—" Bruno barked at Danny. "On the ground. Facedown."

Francie had one heck of a grip on her man, but you could see she wasn't entirely comfortable with the situation. "See, my mom made me take this self-defense course at the Y. She thought it would give me self-confidence. We practiced so often what we'd do if someone came at us from behind, I didn't even think about it." She paused and looked down again at her captive. "You're really getting dirty. I'm sorry, the ground is totally gross. Can you breathe okay?"

Even while she was expressing concern, she didn't loosen her grip one whit.

"Sorry, Danny," the guy on the ground said as Danny lay down next to him.

Then we heard a metallic click. Pam shone her flashlight in the direction of the sound. A man with long gray-streaked hair was standing there in jeans and a plaid shirt. Moonlight gleamed off the barrel of his shotgun.

"All right, kiddies. You've had enough fun for one night. Everybody get off my land. And leave my stock the hell alone."

Danny stood slowly.

Francie got up off her captive and he rolled away. From the front he looked like he'd been dipped in chocolate cake batter.

"We can't exactly leave at the same time," I started to explain to the man.

"Give it a try." He raised the gun.

"No, see, they're Hamilton. We're Lincoln."

Danny had his hands up. "Hey, no problem, man. We're out of here." They backed away, then turned and started running.

We all cheered and hugged and back-slapped. I decided that we'd better introduce ourselves. "I'm Elliot Armbruster," I said. "Head of Find Our Goat. You've probably seen our posters."

"It's been on the radio, too," Francie said. She took off her toque and shook out her hair. I saw what Bruno meant about her hair looking like filaments of copper in the moonlight.

Pam stepped up. She had taken off her toque as well, and her hair flowed over her shoulders. Raw honey, dark and thick. "I'm with the Lincoln High *Sentinel* covering this exclusive story."

Bruno was examining the flashlight left by Danny. I gathered from his expression that it wasn't a bad trophy.

At last the man lowered his gun. "You're with the group offering the reward."

"That's us," I said.

"You're the ones who are giving me all this grief."

"Uh—"

"Actually, that's the Lincoln Alumni Association," Pam said smoothly. She had her pen poised. "You indicated you've been pestered. Do you have a comment for the *Sentinel*'s readers?"

"One that you can print?" He was scowling at all of us. "All right, maybe you better come back to the house."

A friendly black Lab came to meet us as we neared the porch. We decided to leave our boots outside, which meant sitting on the steps and loosening laces at least four feet long. I was wearing white terry-cloth gym socks. There was a small hole in the toe of my left sock, and I tried to pull it forward so no one would see.

Bruno's socks were gray wool. Francie's were pink. Pam's socks were the bright green associated with St. Patrick's Day. Wool, I think. We detective types notice these details.

Bruno was sitting next to me. "This—tonight was a rush," I said. I was wondering if he felt the same way.

"Yeah, well—" He squinted up at the moon. "You can't always count on somebody coming to rescue you like that."

I stared at him. *"Rescue us?* Rescue *us?"* Francie and Pam had been talking, but now they turned to look at us. "We were kicking their butts."

"There were more of them."

Well, sure, I almost said, but you just keep breaking

their arms until they run out of arms. Then you start on their kneecaps. "You mean like maybe somebody might have gotten in a lucky punch."

"Jeez, Armbruster." Bruno stood. "I don't know about you."

We had some skill on our side and some dumb luck, but I hadn't known what I was doing. It was starting to come home to me. I could have gotten hurt.

The man had gone into the house. We could hear him talking to someone inside.

He returned with a woman who looked the same age, around fifty. She wore a poncho over a floor-length flowered dress. He was muttering something about "a bunch of kids playing soldier," but at least he was no longer carrying his shotgun.

She took one look at our green-smeared faces and clapped her hand over her mouth. Her eyes crinkled up like she was laughing. "Are we being invaded? Goodness, I hope you're from a friendly nation."

"Lincoln High." I felt sad. We had been demoted back into schoolkids.

"They're friendly, aren't they, John? Lincoln was always one of my favorite presidents. The log cabin, you know."

"They're the ones responsible for all the hoopla," John answered. "It's their committee. Their reward."

"And their goat."

"Well, yeah. And their goat."

"Perhaps you'd like some granola bars," she offered. "And I can make lemonade. Oh—I'm Rainbow Sangster, and this rude man is my husband, John. He's really very kind except that right now he's disgruntled. Our animals, you know." She reached over to touch his arm. "I think our guests should come inside. Surely anything that has generated such a fuss is worth talking about."

Pam hesitated. "I'm not sure how clean we are."

The surprising thing was that except for a smear of mud on Francie's knee from when she was kneeling on that guy, we were as spotless as when we left home.

I'd spotted the Sangsters as leftover hippies, so I was expecting the floor-to-ceiling loom at one side of the main room. What I didn't expect was all the high-tech gadgetry they had. There was a computer and an entertainment system I'd trade my sister for, if I had a sister.

"Yes, we have all the modern conveniences," John said as if he could read my mind. "Even indoor plumbing."

"Um—" Francie started. "Do you think it would be all right—" She stopped in confusion. "I mean, I'd like to comb my hair." This was a girl who had put a big guy on his face in barnyard manure, and she was too embarrassed to say she had to go.

"Through the hallway," John said. "Past the kitchen."

"I'll show you, dear," Rainbow said.

We all stood around awkwardly. "Well, sit down," John growled after his wife had disappeared with Francie.

One of the couches was leather, so we opted for that one. A fire was crackling away in the brick fireplace and there were oil paintings on the wall, the kind that are just swirls of color but you'd better not say so. "This is great," I said.

Even Bruno looked like he was mellowing.

"So—Mr. Sangster—" I said. "You're having some trouble with your goats?"

"John. Only my mother and the government call me Mr. Sangster. Yeah, right, I'm having trouble with high school kids coming after my animals."

"Has this happened often?" Pam's notebook was resting on her knee.

It had been happening often enough. John detailed the raids that had taken place. He and Rainbow kept forty-eight Angoras for their wool. The goats were friendly, other than the bucks, which tended to be aggressive at that time of year. Reward-seekers were leaving the gates open. Damned hard, John said, to keep any sort of breeding program going with everybody's animals wandering the countryside. An Angora in season didn't give a damn if his lady love was a milk goat.

"We really are trying to find the goat," I said.

"A whole lot of good that's doing me right now," John grumbled.

"If it's any help," Pam said, "we think Linc will be brought to the game against Hamilton next Friday."

John frowned. "It's not like I can stand guard twenty-four hours a day until then. And Rainbow—you've seen her—anybody comes around and she puts something in the oven."

Francie had apparently gone into the kitchen after she finished washing her face and combing her hair. She came out carrying a pitcher of lemonade with fresh mint leaves floating in it. Rainbow followed with a plate of granola bars.

While John went for glasses, Pam borrowed Francie's comb and headed off to the bathroom herself. Personally, I wasn't in a hurry to get rid of the green on my face.

So we were sitting around saying how delicious everything was, and I was thinking about this guy's problems with his goats.

"There's this one goat in particular," John said. "He's

already been nabbed once because he looks so much like your missing goat."

"That's hardly surprising," Rainbow said. "They're very closely related."

"How closely?" Pam asked.

John answered. "They're full brothers, born two years apart. That's Sweetie, by the way." He paused. "Rainbow named him."

Sweetie the Goat. I was getting an idea. "I'm getting an idea," I said.

John poured himself some more lemonade. "It's about time that somebody did." He sat back. "Well, go on. The worst that will happen is that we'll all call you a damned fool."

I suddenly realized that I didn't care if they laughed at me. These were my friends. "I was wondering," I said to John and Rainbow. "Maybe you'd consider lending me a goat for a week."

Nobody laughed.

Okay. This was my brilliant idea. Somebody out there had Linc. Somebody was going to show up on game night to parade Lincoln High's mascot around the stadium wearing Hamilton's colors. Hamilton would have a big laugh at Lincoln's expense. We might end up losing the game because of low morale.

But suppose we said we had the goat? Suppose Paul Horton was willing to identify this goat as the missing one?

He was. John Sangster got on the phone to Horton, who said he'd do anything to stop the raids on his place.

Pam was the only one who balked. "I'm covering

Linc's recovery for the school paper. I can't file a story that's a lie."

"Sure you can," I said, not thinking. "It's easy."

"No, I can't. There's such a thing as journalistic integrity."

"You can't violate your principles," Rainbow agreed.

"Hold on," John said. "The lie wouldn't be for her own advancement."

"It would be in the long run."

I could see my entire plan going down the toilet. "Pam, couldn't you write a story later about how your earlier story helped to recover Linc?"

John's laugh was unpleasant. "You can excuse anything on the basis of the ends justifying the means."

"You're very young," Rainbow told Pam. "I think you should hold on to your integrity."

Pam took a deep breath. "I can ask my teacher, Mr. Farwell. He has to okay everything that goes into the paper, anyway."

Rainbow beamed.

"That's good," John said. "You're never too young to pass the buck."

As for the real Linc—I reasoned that there would no longer be any reason to hold him. Hamilton couldn't very well bring out a second goat because we'd claim that the fake Linc was the real one. The goats weren't about to dispute anything.

The only part I was worried about was how Linc would be released. I didn't think they'd hurt him or anything, but he might be left by the side of the road. I was hoping they'd call the Goatline to say where we could get him. Maybe leave a message of congratulations at the same time.

Goats have this reputation for chewing on everything in sight. After Bruno drove the van up to the house, we put everything from the back into the bench seat area. Pam managed to squeeze herself in there as well. I ended up in back with the goat. I had a wooden box to sit on. No seat belt, of course.

Bruno took the paved road back to town. "How are you doing back there?" he called after we'd gone a few miles.

"Great." Fine. Okay. Nifty. Peachy keen. Right then the goat was going on the carpeting—number one. My boots had been through everything else that night, so what was a little goat pee? At least this goat was neutered, so we didn't end up with a stench guaranteed to attract females from miles around.

Sweetie was well named. I found out that he liked being scratched under his chin. He nudged me with his horns whenever I tried to stop. (It's okay. They're curved back so it wasn't like he could put my eyes out.) He kept trying to investigate my empty pockets, and once he started chewing the bottom of my shirt.

I still wasn't sure where we were going to keep him. I could picture myself bringing him home. *You said I couldn't have a kitten, but you never said anything about a goat.*

So there we were, tooling along, heroes in the making. I could see through the windows in the back door that we were getting closer to town.

Suddenly the back of the car was lit up by flashing blue and red lights, and a siren sounded briefly. "I'm not speeding!" Bruno yelled. "What the—"

Sure enough, we were being pulled over. While we waited for the police, Bruno rubbed his shirt sleeve over his face like he was trying to scrub off the rest of the green. Then he looked at himself in the rearview mirror and gave up.

They were both women, one tall and thin and the other more stocky. As soon as they saw Bruno, they stood back with their hands on their guns.

I couldn't hear very well, but it was clear that Bruno was being asked to step out of the car and keep his hands in sight. The girls got out as well. I was sitting near the floor where I was out of sight. I stood up slightly. "Hello?"

"Cindy!" the taller officer called. "There's another one inside."

"Hey, look—" I stood up as much as I could, which meant that I was leaning over the seat. "I've really got to stay in here. See, if I don't, there could be problems." I was afraid Sweetie might start chewing the upholstery.

"Sonny," the shorter woman said. "Haul it on out of there."

I hauled it on out, keeping my hands up.

They kept us separated. "Look," Bruno was protesting, "I left my wallet at home, okay? I was in a hurry. This is my uncle's truck. He said I could borrow it."

"The vehicle has been reported stolen," the taller woman said. "If you had permission, why would your uncle do that?"

"I didn't tell him. It was a mistake."

"Uh-huh."

"I mean, I should have told him, but he always says I can take the van any time. You can call him."

"Never fear. We will."

171

Francie and Pam both had identification in their purses, and I had my wallet.

"Darla," the shorter woman said, "look at that red hair. Isn't Francine Raines the lawyer's kid? The missing juvenile?"

"My mom's a lawyer," Francie said. "But I'm not missing."

"Not anymore, you're not. You're the one who was running away to get married? Your mama is frantic, do you know that?" Officer Cindy was looking from Bruno to me. "Which one of you boys is the lucky groom?" She flicked my shirt sleeve. "Nice threads to get married in, I must say. And I do admire your limousine. Class all the way."

"Nobody's getting married," Bruno ground out.

"I left a note for my mom," Francie whispered. "Oh, God."

"There's somebody else back there," Officer Darla said. She shone her flashlight in back, then turned. "Cindy, you're not going to believe this. We just hit it big. A missing van, a missing girl, and—are you ready? A missing goat."

Officer Cindy looked as well. She started laughing. "This should be worth a commendation."

"A medal," Officer Darla said. "At the very least."

CHAPTER FOURTEEN

"**E**VERYBODY SMILE for the camera," Bruno's uncle Dom directed.

We were still at the police station, but he had us lined up next to the van with the goat right under MAROS CONSTRUCTION. He looks something like Bruno only a lot shorter and balding and with a long weedy mustache. "Too bad I've already ordered the company's Christmas cards, but this goes with the next ad I put in the newspaper." At least we'd washed the green off our faces.

Once we convinced the police that nothing was stolen, we were hailed as heroes. They seemed gratified that they wouldn't have to search for goats anymore instead of criminals.

While we were having our picture taken, Francie's mother stood nearby in her dark-blue suit and silk scarf. You could tell that Mrs. Raines was not convinced by Francie's explanation for her note. "You know I have poor handwriting. I wasn't going to get married. I was going to a *movie*. Or I thought I was until Elliot told me about the goat." I don't think Francie could have pulled that one off even if she had managed to look her mother in the eye.

"You do not need to pack three suitcases for a movie." Mrs. Raines had decided Bruno was the bridegroom and she wasn't about to back down. "We'll discuss this further at home."

As for Bruno, he totally switched off as soon as Mrs. Raines started talking, as if she were a buzzing insect that wasn't going to sting anybody.

My mom showed up soon after that, just before the reporter from the *Herald*. Mom hugged me as soon as she located me near the van. I felt weird taking her congratulations under false pretenses, but we'd agreed we wouldn't tell the truth to anyone.

The problem was that the police had stopped us before we could get a story together. "Pam has the exclusive story," I told the reporter so we wouldn't contradict each other. We all hung together on that, and everybody refused to say anything else, although we posed for more pictures. Pam hinted to the reporter that we'd used an anonymous source who couldn't be identified for fear of reprisals.

After that, Bruno went off with Sweetie. His uncle said he knew a place to hide the goat for a week.

I took Francie over to the side before she left. "Maybe you should tell your mother about Jason," I said. "She knows something happened." Francie just shook her head.

The thing that didn't make sense was the note Francie left. *I'm getting married.* She had to know that her mother would react big. Why not say she was staying at a friend's house and then phone after she was on her honeymoon? For that matter, why call me?

The message she sent was that she needed help with her suitcases. The one I received was *Help, I'm in over my head*. That's the one I responded to.

"This is the second time today that I've been to the police station," Mom said as we were driving home. "I came earlier about Mrs. Oroville's cats." She thought. "Mrs. Raines is a lawyer. I wonder whether she does pro bono work."

"Pro—what?"

"Some lawyers take certain cases without charge. I spent quite a bit of time today with your Mrs. Oroville. I have her daughter's telephone number, so I'm going to try to contact her. And Mrs. Oroville's family doctor."

I wasn't getting all this. "Hold on."

"Well, you see, Mrs. Oroville's husband wouldn't allow her to have any pets. After his death she took in a kitten, and later a pregnant cat wandered in. Her neighbor—I've spoken to him, and he freely admits that he's been putting down poison. He doesn't like cats in his garden. Apparently there are lots of strays in the area. She's been keeping them inside so they'll stay alive. She stopped taking her medication to feed them all. I suspect a chemical imbalance."

She was talking a mile a minute, her eyes glowing. Maybe she didn't have a career, but my mother had found a cause.

When we got home, the door to the kitchen was closed. "Better open it slowly," Mom cautioned me.

No-Name was in his box next to the stove, lying on a

folded blue towel. He gave a huge yawn when he saw me. I yawned back. It had been a rough night.

Mom poured a cup of cold coffee and put it in the microwave. We both sat at the table. "Are you hungry?" she asked.

I shook my head. "What changed your mind?"

"It was after I talked with Mrs. Oroville. I realized that I could help her. I could really accomplish something. I enjoy dealing with elderly people. They're not all wise and wonderful, but they've lived through so much. Do you see?" I nodded. "Do you?"

"Sure. You want to be a hero, too." I stood as the microwave timer went off. "Is it okay if I take a shower?"

"I think that would be a very good idea."

First I decided to phone Coach.

He was the one who answered the phone, which was good because I still felt embarrassed talking to Melissa.

"Coach? It's Elliot. Armbruster."

"Oh, right." Like he wasn't sure at first who I was. "Look, I'm really impressed with all the work you've been doing to find that goat. I just hope your schoolwork isn't suffering."

"We have him."

Dead silence. "Run that past me again."

"We have the goat."

"Look, son, this goat seems to have a whole lot of look-alikes. I can appreciate that you've been doing your darnedest."

"A tip came over the hot line. I can't tell you the details, but we have the goat back. Paul Horton has positively identified him. The story will be in tomorrow's *Herald*. I thought you should know."

"You're sure that Paul Horton said this goat was the

176

right one?" He paused. "Elliot, I don't mean to doubt you. But we've had so many false leads, I don't want anybody to be let down."

"You can call Mr. Horton." When I spoke to Paul Horton from the Sangster place, I asked him not to tell anybody about Sweetie. That included Coach, who might decide the whole thing wasn't ethical.

"I just may do that," Coach said. "Is this goat safe somewhere?"

"I think so." We had asked the reporter to tell people in his article that the goat wasn't on any of the local farms.

He took a deep breath. "Well—if everybody's going to find out anyway, we'd better make an announcement at school on Monday. Good work, Elliot."

For somebody whose mascot had just been returned, he didn't sound awfully happy.

CHAPTER
FIFTEEN

EVERYBODY loves a hero.

On Monday morning, I was hit by a barrage of congratulations. As goatmania spread like wildfire through the halls of Lincoln High, girls began looking my way and giggling. A freshman girl with long taffy-colored hair dropped her books in front of me and turned bright red when I helped her pick them up. She stammered her thanks, then ran back to where her friends were standing.

"Hey," Lester called when I went to my locker, "how does it feel to be a hero?"

What was I supposed to say? "I'm not a hero."

"Son of a gun." Suddenly Lester had become my pal.

I almost didn't recognize Bruno when I saw him in the hall. He was wearing regular clothes—that is, like everybody else, not army fatigues. Which meant he was wearing jeans with an ordinary shirt open over a T-shirt. He was surrounded by all sorts of girls. Seniors, of course. It figured that I'd get the freshmen.

He looked like he wasn't sure what to do. There were girls ready to hang on his every word, and this was a guy who never had a whole lot of words to spare. So he was standing around looking from one girl to another. It was like he could choose anything he wanted in a bakery. Everything looked good but he wasn't particularly hungry.

When he saw me, he broke free. "Jeez, Armbruster. Everybody's acting weird around here."

"What's with the clothes?" I asked.

He seemed uncomfortable. "See—if my picture's going to be in the paper—I don't know—it seemed like showing off." At first I didn't get it, then I did. Suppose a girl is crowned Miss Peach Blossom and she shows up at school wearing her tiara. Not cool, right? It didn't matter how Bruno normally dressed because nobody had noticed him before.

"Fame changes things," I said.

"No kidding." As he looked around, two girls waved and tossed their hair. He raised his hand slightly in return. The fluttering eyelashes made it look like Lincoln's corridor had an invasion of moths. "I thought you had to play the guitar to get treated like this."

I caught a glimpse of Pam when I passed the journalism room. Martin was sticking so close to her that you'd think they were handcuffed together. I didn't go in. I thought she saw me, but she just frowned and looked away.

In the first *Meat Cleaver High*, the one where Mr. Kramer is stuffed into the locker, a shock wave goes around after the students discover they've killed him. The grads stop speaking to each other. Their shared shame drives a wedge into their friendship.

I felt that Pam was avoiding me.

Aunt Sheila had phoned on Saturday to congratulate me. She asked whether Dev helped very much, and I said he advised me a little at the beginning. I told her about him asking if she had recovered from the shock of macing him. She laughed.

I was thinking about calling Dev, but I decided to wait until the real Linc showed up.

I didn't see Francie until life skills. She came in with some guy talking to her, a senior on the basketball team. Then he seemed to realize that he was in the wrong class-room and backed out.

Bruno was frowning. "Hey, Francie—" he called, but she went straight to her desk. She opened her book and sat there looking like she was reading except without turning the pages.

Basically, Francie looked really good. She was wearing a loose shirt in a violet shade and eyeshadow that seemed all colors, like a guppy. I wondered if she had on one of those lacy things underneath. It's weird when you've known a girl all your life and suddenly she goes female on you. It's like every girl has an alien pod in her closet and at some point the door opens and a woman steps out.

Ms. Winston came in and set her books on her desk. She was carrying a folded newspaper. "I understand that some of you were quite busy this weekend. Mr. Maros, Ms. Raines. And Mr. Armbruster. I was very impressed when I saw your picture in today's paper."

181

Francie's head went up. "Picture?"

There had been a short article in back of the Sunday paper saying the goat had been found.

"Well, yes. I always pick up the first edition on my way to school."

We rushed her desk. There we were with the goat, in front of the van. They had run the picture where Sweetie was nuzzling my hand and I was laughing. Elliot Armbruster—fun guy.

Francie was almost bouncing. More important, she was speaking to us again. Maybe squeaking at Bruno was more accurate. "Look at me! That's me! I look like—"

"A commando?" Ms. Winston offered. Francie nodded gratefully.

"My uncle, man, he's going to buy out the newsstands and send this back to the relatives in Greece."

Ms. Winston cleared her throat. "I don't suppose that one of you would say a few words about what transpired."

That brought us back to reality. "Sorry," I said. "We agreed not to. Some of the details—we have to protect the innocent." Now I sounded like a TV cop.

"Jeez." Bruno scratched his head. "See—no comment, okay?"

Francie didn't say another word, just headed back to her desk and opened her book.

"So who gets the reward?" Lester asked.

Nobody had thought about the reward. "Uh—no comment."

Before the day was over, *no comment* had entered the list with those other handy magic words, *please* and *thank you* and *I'm sorry*.

• • •

After school I finally found Pam without Martin. She was working at one of the tables in the empty journalism room. She glanced up when she saw me. "Oh, hi, Elliot."

I looked behind me to see if her worst enemy had followed me into the room. We were alone. I slid into the chair across from hers. "Are you mad at me?"

She set down her pen. "Why would I be mad at you?"

"I don't know. Why would you?"

In answer, she tore a piece of paper out of the printer. "This is what I've written so far. Read it. *Go on.*"

"Okay." *Sheesh.*

GOAT FOUND. *Friday night four Lincoln students in camouflage gear visited a nearby farm. They were seeking to recover Lincoln High's mascot, an Angora goat named Linc.*

[Here she gave our names.]

The students were following up an anonymous tip left on the goat hot line. Although the tip was bogus, the students didn't return empty-handed.

"Information is everywhere," said Elliot Armbruster. "It's like grass or clouds. Like the air you breathe. And like some of those things, some of it is polluted."

"Did I really say that?" I pointed at the last sentence.

"Yes, you did. You're very poetic at times." She took the paper from my hand and read the rest out loud. " 'This raid was unauthorized by school officials. I was there as an individual, not as a reporter for the *Sentinel*. We left as four individuals and came back as a team with the sort of unity you only read about.' "

"I like that part."

She turned over the page. "Elliot, I won't lie to my readers."

"You're not."

"I'm being deliberately misleading. That's the same thing."

"What did Mr. Farwell say?"

"I didn't tell him. That is, I said I couldn't write about everything that happened. He said he'd leave the story up to my discretion."

"Did you see the picture in the *Herald*?"

She nodded. "I feel so awful about this that my stomach hurts."

"What did you tell Martin?"

"Not much. He wasn't interested in the details. He's just glad it's over." She moved toward the door. "Only it's not."

No goat turned up that day.

Dad had spent the weekend at a conference, so I hadn't seen him since before the raid. He came into the hall when I got home, and for a second I thought he was going to hug me. "Hey," he said, "your mother told me you found the goat, but she never mentioned anything like this." He held up the newspaper, folded to the article about Linc being found. "What do they mean by a commando-style raid?"

I started laughing as I explained. Pretty soon Dad was laughing, too. Mom looked out at us from the kitchen, shook her head, and disappeared again. After I reached the part where John Sangster interrupted things, I sort of slurred over the rest.

"Son of a gun." Dad kept beaming at me. "So you're really doing okay."

I was really doing okay. I'd be doing more okay if the goat showed up.

On Tuesday there was still no news of Linc.

Bruno was wild-eyed when I ran into him in the hall before second period. "A girl asked me to autograph her *arm!* This place is absolutely nutzoid."

"Did you do it?"

"Well—yeah." He grinned and went on to his next class.

By Wednesday our worshippers were dropping off. Mine, anyway. Bruno was still doing okay even though he didn't seem at ease with the girls he was attracting. I kept coming out of class in time to see the same freshman girl immediately turn to face the wall.

"Shelby is waiting for you outside," a guy in band told me just as we were packing up our instruments to leave. As soon as I hit the hall, I caught a glimpse of a plaid skirt disappearing around the corner. So her name was Shelby. I guess I was flattered, only she looked about twelve.

A special edition of the school paper came out with Pam's article. "That it?" Lester complained. "She makes it sound like somebody turned in the goat at the Lost and Found."

"Pam's modest," I said. "Look, we can't talk about it. We were acting on a tip."

He tapped the paper. "It says here your tip was a phony."

"We have a goat, don't we? Trust me. If the truth gets out, somebody might get stomped." Like me.

Except for Pam and her conscience, everybody else was happy. We'd redeemed Lincoln's honor and shamed Hamilton. The big game was coming up on Friday and

185

school spirit had never been higher. Coach told me that special seats had been booked for the four of us in the Reserved area. In other words, we had the best seats on Lincoln's side of the stadium. That was a little rich, even for me. I was just as glad to sit with the band. Pam was one of two school reporters covering the game, so she'd be down on the field. Bruno thought the tickets were great. When Francie didn't say anything, I figured that maybe she wasn't interested, but she just said she hadn't decided whether she wanted to go to the game.

I'm reasonably sure there was a Thursday. I have a dim memory of band practice. Mr. Silverberg thanked me for giving up a seat on the fifty-yard line in favor of staying with the band. He said I had permission to leave after halftime so I could watch the game from a position of privilege. I told him he was welcome to my seat, but he didn't seem to think my offer was serious.

There was some frost on the grass when I woke up Friday morning. I think I'd slept fifteen minutes the whole night.

When I went down to breakfast, Mom said I looked terrible.

"I feel sick."

"It's probably excitement. Tonight's the big game, isn't it?"

"Maybe I shouldn't go."

"Let's see your tongue. Say a-a-ah."

"A-a-ah."

She had a flashlight. When I was a little kid and she looked at my throat, I always expected to see light shining from my fingertips. "Nothing there. You're healthy. Go to school."

End of discussion.

In my own home I'd stopped being a hero really fast. Mom admitted that I'd done okay, only now she was starting to qualify my success. "Of course, that was an animal you found. I don't believe real detectives look for missing animals."

"I'm not a real detective. I'm a kid." I was going to use that as my excuse when I was found out. Youth.

Mom had really been busy that week. She had gone to bat for Mrs. Oroville in a big way, talking to the police and the Humane Society and anybody else who might be able to sort things out with her neighbor. She'd also called Mrs. Oroville's daughter, who didn't believe her at first. Finally the daughter agreed to come out before the end of the month.

In addition, Mom was talking to the Volunteer Bureau about the sort of assistance senior citizens need with their problems. She was already used to dealing with older people through preparing taxes. There are a lot of government agencies, but many people are hesitant to ask for help or don't know whom to ask or how.

I didn't eat any dinner that night. The band was meeting at the school and then being bused over to the stadium. The football team had a separate bus. The air felt charged, everyone was so wired up.

Okay, I realize that all this time I was concerned about the goat, not the game. But that's the way it is. Maybe to the guys who sell hot dogs at the stadium, the game is just a lot of hot dog sales. Maybe the janitors see it as a big mess to clean up. Traffic cops see hundreds of cars spilling out into the night at the same time. For the past two weeks I'd been thinking of nothing but goat. I'd kept up with my homework, but classes and band and sleep had all become spaces between searching for Linc.

It was game time. The band members lined up just outside the field entrance. When Mr. Silverberg gave his signal, we tooted and drummed our hearts out as we marched into a stadium packed almost to the top. There were still some seats at the top of the gray concrete stairs, but even those were filling up fast. The cheerleaders bounced in waving their pom-poms. Graham was doing back-flips, which got a good response. Then Sweetie was led in, wearing the green-and-gold blanket and the leopard skin.

The crowd went wild, cheering and clapping. I'd made all those people happy. Me. I'd done a good thing.

So why was I feeling so lousy?

The goat stopped and looked around curiously, then stayed where he was placed.

I spotted Bruno and Francie up in the good seats. It didn't look like either of them had come with a date, so they were occupying the four spaces reserved for all of us. From what I could see, they seemed to be ignoring each other.

Pam was down at the edge of the field. For the occasion, TV-journalism had trotted out all its equipment. Pam had the microphone, and it looked as if the guy with the camera on his shoulder were on a leash she was holding.

Hamilton's band came in, accompanied by their cheerleaders, who were waving red-and-blue pom-poms.

I held my breath. Their waterboy came in leading . . . a mule.

This couldn't be the same one they'd had years ago because that one was dead. But I had to give Hamilton credit, their mascot looked good. Their side stood and cheered—obviously this was a surprise to everybody.

The teams lined up. I looked at where Bruno and Francie were sitting. Maybe it was my imagination, but I thought they were closer together. They still weren't looking at each other.

I looked out at the field for the kickoff.

It was a good game. When something happened, or something almost happened and everybody stood up, sometimes I turned around to see what Bruno and Francie were doing. By the time the game was really in gear, it looked like they had come together. She was grabbing on to him or they were standing up together and yelling. I mean, that's what you do when something happens to you that's good or bad. You turn to the person closest to you, the one you know best, and you hold on.

At halftime the game was tied, 14 to 14. Each band had a routine to perform and we were on second. We were smooth. Everything went great. I decided that I'd go sit with Bruno and Francie to watch the rest of the game after all.

We were just packing up our instruments when Mr. Silverberg stopped me. "Elliot, stay on the field for a few minutes, will you?" At the same time Mr. Farwell was talking with Pam. He started to take the microphone from her hand. She looked like she was ready to fight him for it. Mr. Silverberg indicated that I should go over to where she was standing. Up in the stands another teacher was talking to Bruno and Francie. She was shaking her head. Uh-uh. No. No way.

So Bruno apparently decided he wasn't going anywhere, either. They stayed where they were. As soon as the teacher left, Francie looked like she was ready to leave. She picked up her purse and she gestured toward the exit stairs. Bruno took hold of her arm and held her there.

By then the principal had come out on the field. She had a big smile like she was running for political office.

I had been herded over to stand next to Pam.

"Oh, God, Elliot," she whispered. "Oh, God-God-God."

The stadium has one heck of an echo, but Mrs. Vizutti's words came through clearly. "Our players aren't the only heroes here tonight. There are four others. I want you to hold your applause until I finish introducing them. "Pamela Culhane—"

After a moment's hesitation, Pam held up one hand. "I think I hate you." She spoke in a low enough voice so I was the only one who could hear her.

"—Bruno Maros—" Bruno didn't hesitate at all. He gave a big grin and held up the arm that he wasn't using to keep Francie with him, making a clenched-fist salute. I didn't know what was happening with Francie. Then Bruno said something to her. At first she looked at him peculiarly. She nodded.

"—Francine Raines—" I was almost expecting Francie to bolt when Bruno let go of her. Instead she gave this nervous smile and held up both hands high, V for victory. Her smile grew, became real. Bruno started laughing.

"—Elliot Armbruster—" Pam had backed away.

I stepped out and held up both arms. The stadium went wild. The Lincoln High crowd was cheering while some Hamilton kids booed. I turned around and around, like a pig on a spit. I kept on turning while flames licked at my belly.

CHAPTER
SIXTEEN

WE WON, 31 to 20. That night victory parties were held all over Lincoln's side of town. Usually my social calendar isn't exactly overflowing. There were houses where I could go after the games with other band members. But that night I was invited to places I ordinarily wouldn't be. When the band was packing up, a girl I recognized as a friend of Shelby's asked where I was going. "Anywhere I want," I answered.

I thought she looked disappointed.

I don't know where Pam went or whether Francie and Bruno stayed together. I went to this guy's house where I hardly knew anybody and everybody was whooping it up except me. I ended up phoning my dad for a ride home. If you want to know the truth, it wasn't such a great night.

I didn't want to think about the goat anymore, so I spent the rest of the weekend catching up with two weeks' worth of taped TV shows. I wanted to see real heroes solve crimes in an hour, less commercials. I wanted guaranteed success.

For once Mom didn't bug me.

On Sunday afternoon Dev called. "Hey," he said, "I understand that congratulations are in order. Good job."

"Thanks." I had picked up the call in the den, so I was able to talk. "Only we don't exactly have the goat. Yet."

"What was that in the newspaper picture? A loaner?" He laughed.

"Well, yeah."

He stopped laughing. "Sorry?"

I told him what we did. I told him I'd figured Hamilton was avoiding embarrassment by keeping Linc until after the game. Now the game had been over two days, Sweetie was back home, and the goat still hadn't been returned. The whole thing sounded lame, even to me. "See, we were running out of time."

Dev didn't say anything at first. When he did, he seemed to be choosing his words carefully. "Elliot, I realize that you were helping out your school. Only you should understand something. Investigators investigate. They look for truth. They don't go around granting wishes. That's for fairy godmothers."

I had to swallow before the words would come out. "You're saying that I messed up."

"That depends on what you wanted to accomplish."

"I wanted to see if I could do it—be a detective." Like you, I almost said.

His voice was gentle. "Elliot, most people start with routine matters. Your problem is that you got impatient. You went creative."

He was being nice about it, but he was saying that

when I didn't get the results I wanted, I had made up my own.

"What do you think I should do?"

"How many people know about the substitution?"

There were the four of us, and Mr. and Mrs. Sangster, and Paul Horton. "Seven. Eight, including you." Maybe Mrs. Horton, too.

"That's quite a few people to keep a secret. I'm surprised it hasn't leaked out already." He paused. "You might consider issuing a statement yourself before the truth comes out. 'I did it for old Lincoln High.' Right now that's the best I can come up with. You and your friends should prepare to receive some flak. I don't know why, but a lot of people like to see their heroes go up in flames."

I groaned.

"Still," he went on, "it wasn't a bad bluff. If nothing else, Coach Garvey should be grateful. Some players are superstitious in a big way. Coach is, too. All he needed was for something bad to happen to the Lincoln mascot before the big game. A lot of the guys would consider it an omen."

Then I remembered. "Coach Garvey said I should give you a message."

"He did? What is it?"

"He said, 'Tell him that Coach is truly astounded.' "

"He said that? Those words?" Dev started laughing. "I don't believe it."

"What did he mean?"

"Don't worry about it." He hesitated. "All right, I'll tell you. When I was in school, a joke yearbook came out at the same time as the real one. The joke book had predictions about everybody's future. I was supposed to wind up in a maximum security prison. It was a joke, but there were a few teachers who agreed. Coach told me he'd be truly astounded if that prediction didn't come true."

"Maximum security—for stealing a mule?"

He sucked in his breath. "He told you about that?"

This was the first I'd known for sure. I should have figured it out from the way Dev's face lit up every time he mentioned that earlier theft. "He hinted."

Dev was silent for a moment. "The reward is two hundred dollars. Is that much to kids these days?"

"It's a lot to some."

"You'd think the goat would have shown up by now. Look," Dev offered before we hung up. "I still know some guys I went to school with. I'll nose around a little and see if anyone has heard anything. But don't hold your breath."

I promised not to. Only living people could hold their breath. I was a dead man.

It was raining on Monday. I hadn't finished my life skills paper, but it wasn't due for a week. I figured on asking Bruno if he wanted me to look at his paper when he was finished or if he needed more help. We'd only been partway done that night when we were interrupted by Pam's call.

I was just putting my books in my locker when a girl cleared her throat. I looked up to see Francie's violet plastic raincoat. Next to her stood Pam, in black vinyl. Across the hall my freshman was watching us with wide eyes.

Both Francie and Pam looked serious. "What's happening?" I asked as I shut my locker.

"Mr. Farwell just told me," Pam said. "On Wednesday

196

there's going to be a victory rally. They're presenting the check to us."

"Check?" At first I couldn't figure out what check she was talking about.

"It wouldn't be right for us to accept the reward."

Francie nodded.

"We could donate it to some charity," I suggested. I noticed that although Shelby had looked like she was actually planning to speak to me, she had just left.

"Greenpeace is good." Francie bit her lip. "Sorry."

"It isn't our money to give," Pam said quietly.

Uh-oh.

Francie's next words confirmed my worst suspicions. "She's going to tell, Elliot."

Nuts.

Aunt Sheila always says that when I want something, I have eyes like a cocker spaniel. I looked pleadingly at Pam. "I need more time. The goat is going to turn up. I want to check out some old Hamilton grads."

She shook her head. "I have to explain why we can't accept the check."

I groaned. "Is this absolutely necessary?"

"For me it is," she said. "Yes."

I managed to talk her into waiting another day. She told me she was preparing a story explaining the situation, which would come out in next week's paper.

"I tried, Elliot," Francie said as Pam left for class. "You know, I never thanked you for the other night, with Jason. That could have been bad."

"That's okay."

"I couldn't convince my mom that I had been plan-

197

ning to see a movie. I finally told her the truth. Her reaction wasn't great."

"What's she going to do? Ground you?"

"We're going to see this family counselor. So—I don't know. Maybe it won't be so bad."

"Maybe things will get better."

"Maybe I don't care." I blinked at her, surprised. "Maybe I've always cared too much what my mother thinks. Only Friday when we were all there at the farm— I'm not a total washout, you know?"

"Yeah?"

"Yeah. Hey, maybe Bruno—" She stopped. "Pam won't listen to Bruno."

That reminded me of something I'd been wondering about. "Francie, at the game, when they were calling our names, you looked like you wanted to leave. What did Bruno say to you?"

"Nothing special," she answered quickly. "I don't remember. Maybe that it looked like a good game and we had good seats." Even in kindergarten Francie had never been able to get away with lying. I think it comes with having skin that's almost transparent. She looked at her watch. "I've got to go. If I can do anything to help—well, you know."

I knew.

Around me swirled the last-minute rush of students heading to their classes. Everybody smelled like wet dog. I watched Francie disappear around the corner.

It was Monday now. The victory rally was Wednesday.

That meant I had two days to find the real goat.

"No big deal," Bruno said when I told him about Pam. We were having lunch together in the cafeteria, which meant we were yelling. Since everybody else was doing the same thing, our conversation was as private as if we were alone on the moon. "Hey, it's going to be a relief, you know, figuring out if any of these girls like me for real. They've been calling the house—my dad's starting to get ticked off. And my mom, she's really old-fashioned. She doesn't like girls calling at all."

I wasn't sure that Bruno understood. "It doesn't bother you that we're going to look like complete frauds?"

He was chewing on a sandwich, so he shook his head.

"I'm thinking about changing schools," I said.

He swallowed. "Why?"

"I've messed up everything here. After this, Elliot Armbruster is going to be another name for death on a stick."

"You want to take a walk?" Bruno wadded up the brown bag from his lunch. "Come on, let's get out of here."

The rain had stopped, but not many people were outside, so we pretty well had the school grounds to ourselves.

"You know your problem, Armbruster?" Bruno asked after we stopped near the fields. A thick mist was rising up. "Your problem is that you're too serious. You and Pam, you're a lot alike that way."

"Pam's a pain in the butt." That was another thing that bugged me. I'd gotten involved in this whole thing trying to impress her. Trying to impress myself. "Why aren't you bothered?"

He shrugged. "Because I'm not. We did okay."

"We didn't do okay. We *said* we did okay. There's a difference."

"Why?"

"Why?" I was incensed. *"Why?"*

"Armbruster, look at it this way. If we'd gone to that farm and the goat had been there—"

"The goat wasn't there."

"If the goat had been there, we would have taken it. I have no doubt about that whatever. We might have suffered some losses, but we would have had that goat. Pam would have written her story."

The goat hadn't been there, we hadn't taken him, there had been no losses, and Pam's article was full of evasions. Otherwise, I followed his logic. "Okay."

"What I'm saying is that we're not looking at complete failure here."

"You're not looking at complete failure. It was my responsibility to find the goat. I never got anywhere near it."

"Armbruster, football season is over. Nobody cares about the goat anymore except you and Pam." His expression had become more serious. "You did everything you could. You asked around, right? You started the hot line. Those posters—that was you. Have you been doing anything these past two weeks except looking for that goat?"

"Band practice," I said. "I went to band practice."

"So what do you really have to kick yourself about, other than lying and that kind of stuff? You tried like hell. Maybe you didn't get results, but . . . tough."

Maybe if I had succeeded once as a detective, I'd buy what he was saying. "What will your folks say when they find out?"

"Nothing. I told my uncle Dom because he wanted details. He said that was fine."

"He didn't mind?"

"It takes a lot to get Uncle Dom bent out of shape. Sure, it was fine with him. The publicity is still good. Oh, yeah—he said you must be really intelligent to think up such a plan."

I wasn't about to touch that one. "I was wondering. What did you say to Francie at the game when she wanted to leave?"

"Oh, that." He scratched his nose. "I told her that if she behaved herself, maybe I'd take her to a movie some-time."

"No kidding?"

He looked at me like he couldn't believe I was taking him seriously. "Sure, I'm kidding. I told her what I just told you."

"And she bought it?"

"It's true. She didn't have anything to apologize for. Jeez, I wish it hadn't been so dark so I could've seen that guy's face when Francie put him on the ground. I couldn't have done much better myself. Except I wouldn't have apologized. She was great. I guess nobody had ever told her that before."

"Do you think you might take her out sometime?"

An uncertain expression came over his face. "Uh . . . I think she likes older guys."

"You're older."

"Not that much older. How do you think I'd look with a beard?"

"Hairy."

This time I dodged out of his reach before he could punch my shoulder.

Bruno was still hungry, so he took off to see what was left in the cafeteria. I decided to take one last walk around the area where Linc had disappeared. The football field. The bushes where he'd browsed. I stopped at the tree where he had been tied. Anybody could have driven in there. *Anybody.* I bashed my fist against the tree and an icy blob of water fell straight down the back of my neck.

The ground felt spongy underfoot as I left the dripping trees and headed onto the fog-bound playing field. It was like moving through cotton candy, breathing it in, letting it go straight through my body. My clothes stuck to me, damp and uncomfortable, but I kept walking—getting nowhere, going nowhere. Overhead, the sun shone like a dim lightbulb. All I could see were the blurred outlines of trees. Beyond the trees, the world ended.

I stopped at the goalposts and stood there, shivering. Life Skills had taught me an important lesson: He who spreads his wings can expect to go down in flames. I pressed my eyes shut tightly. Never, I promised myself. Never again.

Never. Never. Never.

"Kill him—kill him—kill him—"

The crowd was getting restless. I was back on the field, like on the night of the game, only this time I stood alone. "It looks like we have a penalty." The voice from the commentator's booth sounded like Uncle Ed on Radio FM 99.6. "Elliot Armbruster has been called for lying. And what's the penalty for lying?"

"Lion—lion—lion—"

In front of the bleachers, the cheerleaders waved their pom-poms. The band played the Funeral March.

"Oh, come on," I protested. "You can't kill a guy for—" I staggered back as a deep roar shook the trees. Mr. Silverberg lowered his baton.

The beast, giant and tawny, approached from the other side of the field. He spotted me and shook his mane.

"Nice kitty," I said, then stopped as he roared again, showing gleaming yellow teeth. This was one mean cat.

A powerful car slammed out of the fog onto the field. "Grab cover, kid!" a familiar voice yelled. "I'm coming to get you!"

"Dan?"

He stood there on the ten-yard line with a semiautomatic rifle in each hand. "Hey, kid," he said out of the corner of his mouth. "Long time no see."

The crowd screaming for my blood had faded away. Lola got out of the Mercedes to pet the lion. She saw me and waved. Her golden hair shimmered over her shoulders.

Dan squinted at me. "My sources say you tried solving a case on your own. My sources say you fell on your butt."

"I tried, Dan," I told him. "I asked questions. I probed." I'd investigated my heart out.

"Yeah?" He seemed mildly interested. "And what happened when you put everything together?"

Put everything together? "Nothing fit together."

"Huh." He shrugged. "That's okay. Some have it and some don't. So now you know." He shifted the guns around and looked at his watch. "I gotta go. The bald man's out of the joint again and he's gunning for Lola. I just wanted to remind you that we're still around if you get bored." He began to turn away. "Stick with me and you'll never fail."

Lola looked back at me as she got into the car. Her lips formed words that I couldn't read. She blew a kiss.

With a screech of tires, they were gone.

I was on my way back toward the class buildings when I spotted Shelby standing at the edge of the field. My one and only groupie. She turned away when she saw me looking at her.

"Hey, wait!" I called.

She stopped and pointed to herself questioningly. I nodded. I wasn't sure what I wanted to say to her as I hurried in her direction. Something like she should head into the nearest lifeboat because I was a sinking ship.

She waited for me even though she couldn't meet my eyes once I reached her. "Oh, hi, Elliot."

We had never actually spoken. "Hi, Shelby. Are you heading to class?"

She nodded. "I've been wanting to say congratulations on finding the goat."

"I don't think you should exactly congratulate me." I'd just appreciate it if she didn't throw any rocks. I'd taken a chance, and soon everyone would know that I'd lost.

"I'd been worried that he might be sick," she said. "He wasn't, was he?"

"Why did you think he was sick?"

She licked her lips. "It was the way he was lying next to that tree where he was tied."

"You saw him—on the day he disappeared?"

Her eyes widened, I guess because my voice had gotten louder. "Uh-huh. My parents know some people with a farm, and that's not the way goats usually look when they're sleeping. He was just lying there, but he didn't look right at all."

"Was he moving?"

She shook her head. "I didn't even see him breathe."

In *Track Meat*, which is *MCH* 35 or 36, high school athletes are being killed in disgusting ways with gym equipment. One runner disappears after the first murder.

All during the rest of the movie, everybody looks for him because they know he was under heavy pressure to win. They think a bad reaction to taking steroids is causing him to kill his rivals. His girlfriend keeps saying that he isn't really evil.

She's right. He's really dead.

"You haven't seen my gray kitty, have you?"

"Some of the players are superstitious in a big way."

"I don't believe either of these goats is the right one."

I had it. I stared at Shelby. "You're beautiful."

Then I turned and took off at a run toward the gym.

Coach was sitting at his desk, for once not talking on the phone. I rapped on the door and he motioned for me to come in. He didn't look entirely pleased to see me. "Well, Elliot, what did you think of the game?"

"Great."

"Sit down." I sat. "I guess you might say that it's time for us to sever our relationship." He waited. "Find Our Goat? No more reason for that anymore, is there?"

"I have a theory about the goat," I said.

He leaned back. "Elliot, I'm real glad you found that animal, but I don't think I need any more theories. His reappearance was more than enough."

This was not like TV. On TV there's always somebody to lead the bad guy off to jail. On TV the bad guy is really a bad guy, not a good guy doing a bad thing for what probably seemed a good reason. On TV the bad guy can't make you run laps.

I took a deep breath. "The goat at the stadium Friday wasn't Linc. He was a substitute I brought in. I think the real Linc is dead. I think he's been dead from the start."

Coach stood up and made sure the door was closed. He returned to his desk. "Go on."

"I know a lot of football players are superstitious. Having our mascot die before the big game might be considered bad luck."

"Might be the kiss of death." His eyes had gone cold.

"Someone had to take the body away. The players were all practicing on the field. So it had to be someone with the right kind of vehicle, someone who left before everybody else did."

He held up his hands to indicate time out. "All right, we both know you're a smart boy. This theory of yours—what's the point? I'm assuming you can't prove any of it."

So I told him. I told him that Pam was upset about losing her journalistic integrity and she was writing an article. I told him how many people knew about Sweetie, that the substitution wouldn't stay a secret. I didn't accuse him of taking the dead goat. I didn't have to.

The weird thing was that I was almost positive that I was the one who had given him the idea of claiming that Hamilton had stolen the goat. Linc had only been missing until I brought up the earlier theft and what it had done for morale. Coach himself must have made the call to the radio station.

After I finished, he just sat there. Finally he spoke. "What do your friends say about this theory of yours?"

"I haven't told them. Like you say, there's no point. See, it's going to come out that we lied. We need some credibility. We need to show that we're responsible for finding the goat, even if he's dead. To do that, we need a body."

"A body." He winced. "It's been two weeks. Do you know what a buried body is like after two weeks?"

The weather was cool, but the ground was a long way from frozen. "I guess I'm going to find out."

"Better you than me," he muttered. He stood, so I did, too. "All right. I'll see if I can do anything. Oh—is that hot line of yours still open?"

"I think so."

He nodded.

I went out of his office, but I was back a minute later. "Class has already started. I need a hall pass."

Wordlessly he scrawled off a note from a pad on his desk.

"Thanks, Coach."

"Don't mention it." He looked me square in the eye as he handed over the pass. *"Not ever."*

CHAPTER
SEVENTEEN

IT WAS ALMOST dinnertime when Pam phoned. She sounded excited, almost like her old self. "There's been a call on the Goatline."

Me, innocent: "What kind of call?"

She played it back to me. The voice sounded like an old codger. He'd been out of town awhile, so he missed all the hullabaloo. Two weeks earlier he'd found the body of a goat near Lincoln High. No marks on it, but the animal was dead. He didn't think it was right to leave something like that around where children might see it, so he buried it in a nearby construction site. He gave the location, including the corner of the lot. He wasn't interested in any reward.

"That was an adult's voice, Elliot."

"Well, that's great." I was trying to sound enthusiastic, but my mind was squeezed dry, like a lemon.

"Elliot, *this might be it*."

She picked me up a few minutes later and we drove

by the site. It was already dark, so all we could see was a vacant lot where the ground was being prepared for construction. For a minute I expected her to suggest we start digging by flashlight, like we were going for worms (which I definitely didn't want to think about). "Looks good," I said as she drove me home.

"You phone Bruno. I'll get Francie. Then—tomorrow—we'll go after school. Oh, God, I hope this is it."

Me, too.

The only difficulty I could see was that this was somebody's job site. We couldn't just walk in and start digging holes. As it turned out, Bruno's uncle Dom had friends involved in the construction project. He arrived in his truck and some workers lent us their backhoe for a few minutes. I thought Bruno was showing off for Francie when he operated it. If so, it didn't work because she was watching everything in a cool, detached way. Or maybe she had caught on that Bruno's feelings were mixed about girls who threw themselves in his path.

The body was wrapped in a blue tarp. We opened it far enough to confirm there was a goat inside. Pam and I both turned shades of green, but at least we were green together. Pam's mother's veterinarian friend had agreed to look at the body to see if she could determine the cause of death, so all that was left was to wait for her findings.

I called Dev when I got home that night. "I found him," I said. "The goat. I did it." I wouldn't tell him how or who did it or why, but I had to tell somebody who understood.

"The real goat this time?" He sounded cautious.

"The real goat. The news isn't good, and you won't know it's me when you hear about it—see, nobody else knows that I figured it out. There's this one guy, but we made a deal." I stopped. "I guess you don't have any way to know I'm telling the truth."

"Sure I do."

That stopped me. "How?"

"Because you refused to be congratulated the first time. And you're not giving up your source. And because this time you sound like you accomplished something. Congratulations, Elliot."

I deserved that.

"Elliot—that aunt of yours—"

"Aunt Sheila?"

"The one who maced me. Is she going with anybody or anything like that?"

"She's engaged," I said. "She gets engaged all the time."

He didn't say anything for a minute. "Give me a call the next time she gets unengaged."

Wow.

The vet didn't have any trouble figuring out why the goat died. Apparently Linc found a small apple and he choked to death.

On Wednesday Paul Horton appeared at the rally. He spoke last, after the players were applauded and Coach told the students they'd done a great job cheering the team on to victory.

Then Paul stood up. He told everybody in the school auditorium that Linc had reached a good age for a goat. His death was nobody's fault, and the things that happened after that were partially the result of a misunderstanding. He didn't mention our names, but everybody knew who he was talking about when he said we'd done all the goat owners in the area a service.

After that the student body president called for a minute of silence for Linc. She said that she'd spoken with the head of the alumni association and they wanted to donate the reward money to the SPCA in the school's name.

A special victory cheer was led for the players, and the assembly ended. Since it was the end of the day, everybody was heading to their lockers or out the door.

Shelby and her friends were a couple of rows down from where I was sitting. We ended up clumped together in the crowd waiting to get out. "Hi," I said.

Her eyes were accusing. "You lied."

"That's right."

Her girlfriend was tugging her to go down a row of seats to the other aisle. She hesitated. "Did you lie about everything?"

I wasn't sure what she was talking about. "No, not about everything."

Then Lester came up to me, and she was gone. I was out of the auditorium before I figured out she was asking if I'd lied when I said she was beautiful. What I'd meant was *Thank you. A lot.*

Bruno and Francie were waiting out in the hall. Bruno looked like he'd been sweating, so maybe this whole thing had bothered him more than he admitted. Francie's freckles were darker than usual, but her color seemed to be coming back. All Bruno would say was "Things could have been worse."

"It's over," Francie said. "I haven't heard anybody say anything really bad."

"I did," I said. "Lester told me he would have done exactly the same thing."

We found Pam in the journalism room. She was sitting at a computer, all alone. We gathered around and waited for her to notice us.

She stopped typing. "Are you guys still speaking to me?"

Bruno spoke up. "It's not your fault if you have integrity. You just need to lighten up a little." He wiped his forehead. "Jeez, I feel like I need a shower. Did anybody else notice how hot it was in the auditorium?"

"I felt cold," Francie said.

"Cold," Pam said.

"I was paralyzed—I didn't feel a thing." I looked around. "Where's Martin?"

Pam didn't react at all. "That's hard to say." She and Francie exchanged glances. I began to get the drift that I had missed something.

"I was thinking maybe the four of us could go and get some shakes or something," I said. "A victory toast."

"Which victory?" Pam asked.

Francie answered first. "All of them."

At home I thought I'd better tell Mom and Dad the truth about the goat before they heard it somewhere else. They didn't seem to know how to react. This was obviously not a situation Mom had run into in any parenting class. Help came from an unexpected source when Coach called them and the other parents to say they shouldn't be too hard on us because we had helped a lot of people.

So that part was okay.

• • •

Mrs. Oroville's daughter flew in from New York as she promised. Mom spent a lot of time driving them around, mostly because she wanted to be there in case Noreen tried to put Mrs. Oroville into a home for crazy people without examining the situation. However, once Noreen found out that Mrs. Oroville had been neglecting her medication, she concentrated on getting her mother well again.

Mrs. Oroville's house was another problem. It smelled, all right, but the cats had been well cared for. Noreen told Mom that her mother had always hated the heavy furniture picked out by her husband. She wasn't at all surprised to find the living room turned into a claw-sharpening area. Mrs. Oroville did have more money, by the way. It was locked up under the terms of her husband's will. Francie's mom helped with that part.

Anyway, before Noreen returned to New York, she and her mother began to make plans to redecorate, which included covered fencing in a section of the yard. Noreen hired a nurse companion for Mrs. Oroville—one who likes animals. She also opened an account with the vet for cat examinations and neutering.

The weird part about this whole thing is that without even being in Ms. Winston's class, my mom unfurled her sails and set off on her own voyage of discovery. She has just enrolled in a college program on advocacy, which deals with speaking up on behalf of other people.

Mom tried something called a jambalaya the other day, which is a sort of rice and seafood casserole. It was really good, her first experiment that worked out.

• • •

We still had to finish our assignment for life skills class. These are some sections from our papers:

Francie: I used to think that if I did something to help the planet, people would look up to me because I was doing important work. Maybe that's true. But one thing I learned is that people who help the planet are not necessarily people who are nice to other people. Maybe some of them are even good to trees because trees are easier than people.

I still want to help the planet, but now it's because our planet needs all the help it can get. I also think that people are fine.

Bruno: The reason you need a profesional army is that otherwise what you end up with is guys hitting each other with sticks. A strong proffesional army keeps things from getting dumb so everybody doesn't get killed.

Me: A month ago I said I wanted to be a detective. When I said that, I really meant I wanted to look like a TV detective. That was my first mistake. Real detectives don't look like TV stars. They don't act like them, either.

A detective looks at a problem like a jigsaw puzzle. He takes it apart and examines the pieces, then sees how the pieces fit together from all sides. This takes time. Sometimes it's boring.

I tried to solve a mystery like a detective . . . at first. I made my second mistake when I decided to take a shortcut. This is like doing a jigsaw puzzle by jamming the pieces together. All you do is wreck the pieces.

Pam wrote an article that appeared in the school paper after the rally. This is part of what she said:

I've always heard that the ends do not justify the means. That means you can't do whatever you want because you believe it's for the best. Some very bad things have been justified that way.

Reporters must report the truth as they see it.

She apologized without groveling too much. Then she got on with writing for the paper. She says this experience will make her a better journalist.

Pam isn't seeing Martin anymore, by the way. She told Francie that they decided to see other people because they didn't seem to have much in common. So far, this seems to mean that Martin is seeing other people. Pam says she wants to concentrate on her schoolwork for a while.

Last Friday the four of us went to a movie. That was as friends, not like dating, although I know for a fact that Bruno has taken out Francie at least once. Pam didn't seem to mind being seen with a younger guy—she didn't act like she was baby-sitting or anything.

The picture was the latest *Meat Cleaver High*. It was the best one so far, the sort of picture where girls grab on to you but they don't get sick or spill your popcorn.

I'll tell you about it sometime.